"Josette and Caleb"

by
Geri Blackwell-Davis

airleaf.com

Also by
Geri Blackwell-Davis

"In The Lion's Den"

Coming soon

"Tena's Terror"

This book is dedicated to my family and friends. Without their encouragement to continue writing, this book "Josette and Caleb," would not have been written. After reading my first novel "In The Lion's Den" they wanted more.
I thank you all.

Geri Blackwell-Davis

Chapter 1

Josette is fishing at Blue Mountain Lake, her favorite place in the world. Here she feels at peace. The hectic life she led when she was younger is over. She raised two daughters alone after her husband died. They were eight and ten years old at that time. It was hard looking white and being married to a colored man in the South. However, she had his protection and respectability while he was alive. The colored men of Willow Park, kept their distance because of him. A few tried to entice her into their beds but they only tried it once. She told her husband Wyn Fuller, and he put a stop to it immediately. Because she looked white and was beautiful, white men lusted after her too but in a disrespectful way. They knew she wasn't white. She never told Wyn about these men. She was afraid for his life because they lived on the edge of a Klan dominated town in rural South Carolina. She never told him how they would whoop and yell at her when they saw her on the street. They knew who her husband was and only yelled at her when she was alone. Some of the language they used was disgusting. She lived in fear of both colored and white men. After giving birth to two pretty girls very light in color, her fear increased as they grew older.

She had seen Caleb Carter fishing at the lake on many occasions. Whenever she saw him, she would go in the opposite direction. She thought he didn't see her. He did though and dismissed her from his mind. He thought of her as just another person enjoying a day of fishing. He never got close enough to see who she was.

Their meeting is accidental. Caleb usually wears hip boots and wades out to deeper water to fly fish. The lake is big but it isn't very deep until you reach the middle. There, it's deep enough to be dangerous if one is not able to swim. Today, Caleb didn't want to fish. He only wanted to relax. Maybe later he would try his hand at fishing. He makes a pillow of his jacket and lies on the grass away from the shore. The sky is clear and azure blue with wispy white clouds floating by. The day is comfortably warm and Caleb drifts off to sleep with a feeling of contentment.

Josette is walking around the lake looking for a good spot to set her pole and fish. She never wades in the water. She likes to prop up her pole and watch it bounce when a fish takes the bait.

Caleb has been asleep about thirty minutes when she comes to where he is. She can't see him because of some bushes growing between him and the lakeshore. She sets her pole and waits. She hums to herself. Her favorite songs are hymns. Her favorite hymn is *"Breathe On Me Breath Of God."* This beautiful melody stays in her head all the time and she hums or sings it to herself every day.

Caleb wakes to this beautiful tune being sung softly by a beautiful woman sitting on a blanket. Her back is to him, her knees are drawn up and her chin is resting on them. Her eyes are closed and she is at peace with her surroundings and herself. Caleb is fascinated and wonders who she is. He can't see her face. He can only see her long dark brown hair hanging down her back. He watches her for a few minutes thinking, what a beautiful sight. I wonder who she is. He doesn't want to startle her so he moves quietly as he approaches her and softly says, "That's a mighty pretty song Miss." His caution is useless. She jumps, almost falls over and knocks her pole down.

"I'm sorry Miss I didn't mean to scare you."

"Where did you come from? I didn't see you. If you're fishing here I can leave." She starts to reel her line in.

Caleb very quickly says, "Oh no, don't go! I wasn't fishin'. I was just restin' back there. I guess I fell asleep. It's so pretty and peaceful here. Please stay. If you don't mind I'll set up over there. This Lake is big enough for two people to fish at the same time. I'm Caleb Carter from Lylesville."

"Well if you don't mind Caleb, I'll stay. I like this section of the lake. I come here often. What about you? Do you fish here often too?"

"I sure do but I've never been to this section before. I stumbled on it accidentally today and found it so pretty; I decided to stay. Now that the company is pretty too, I may never leave."

Josette is surprised. Caleb is flirting with her. She knows who he is but evidently he doesn't know her. She makes no reply and pretends she doesn't hear him.

The conversation stops while Caleb sets up his pole. They settle down to wait for a hungry fish to come along. It's quiet and peaceful and every now then Caleb looks over at Josette. He can't keep his eyes from looking her way. He thinks she is the most beautiful woman he has ever seen. Then, Josette gets a bite on her line and her pole is almost dragged into the lake. She was daydreaming when the pole fell. She and Caleb run to the water's edge to get the pole before it disappears. Caleb gets there first.

Josette is jumping up and down yelling, "Get it. Get it."

He grabs the pole and tries to reel in whatever is on the line. It's very heavy and the pole is bending too much so he drops the pole and starts to pull on the line.

Caleb says, "I don't think this is a fish. It's too heavy."

Josette is yelling, "Ease up Caleb, ease up. It's only a five-pound test line. It may break." Suddenly a big black snapping turtle comes up out of the water with the line in his mouth. Josette runs back up the bank away from Caleb and the turtle yelling "Cut him loose. He'll bite. Be careful he'll bite."

Caleb is trying his best to stay away from the turtle's long neck and open mouth. He's surprised at its size. The turtle is huge. "Get me somethin' to cut the line. Hurry, throw me a knife or somethin' hurry up!"

Josette runs to where she was sitting and gets a scaler and throws it to him. "That's all I've got."

Caleb looks like he is dancing with the turtle, trying to dodge his long neck and open mouth. The scaler Josette threw him is dull and he is having a hard time trying to cut the line and dodge the turtle at the same time. Finally the line breaks. The turtle, realizing he is free of the crazy creature he was tied to, hurries back to the safety of the water.

Josette and Caleb fall on the ground laughing. "Man oh man, that was one mad turtle. I thought he was gonna get me a couple times."

Josette is still laughing, "I did too. You and that turtle looked like you were dancing. I've never seen one that big before. I didn't know they grew that big and I've never seen one in this lake."

"I've never seen one that big either." Caleb is still laughing. "You were no help, throwin' me a dull scaler and runnin' away like that."

Josette can't stop laughing. "I'm sorry, I only saw something big and black suddenly fly up out of the water. I didn't know what it was. The surprised look on your face was priceless but I must say, you sure know how to move your feet."

Josette and Caleb try to go back to fishing but every time they look at each other they laugh. The image of Caleb dancing with a turtle was a funny sight.

Chapter 2

The Spinner brothers go to Blue Mountain Lake too. They have been there camping and fishing for a week. They drink moonshine, cook and eat the fish they catch and annoy other people trying to relax and fish.

Josette knows who they are and when she sees them at the lake, she packs up and leaves before they see her. Their presence spoils her peaceful day. She isn't the only one who leaves. Other people trying to fish or wanting to relax on the shore also leave. No one wanted to be around these two loud mouth, foul smelling drunks. Today the Spinners chose to annoy people on the other side of the lake. They didn't see Josette.

They know her though. When they see her in town shopping, they yell disgusting words at her. "Hey Josette, pull up that dress and let me see if you the same color all over." They slap each other on the back laughing. "Hey Josette, what color is your coochie? Can we see it?"

Whenever she goes out, she is constantly on guard. These men cause an abnormal fear in her, it's more than just being afraid of them. It's something deeper. She doesn't know what it is. If she sees them first, she changes her direction by going around corners or hiding in stores until she feels safe. Avoiding them wastes a lot of time and makes her very angry. She is terrified when her two girls are with her.

All of her young years were hard because of how she looked. It was hard growing up in a small town in the south being colored and looking white but it made her tough.

When she was in elementary school, she and her friends would be walking home and the white kids would yell at them. "Oh look! It's gonna rain dark clouds a comin'." Then they would run away laughing. Josette wanted to run after them and beat them up but her friends held her back. "Let them go Josette. They ain't worth us gettin' in trouble over. They just a bunch of dumb crackers anyway." Eventually she learned to ignore those remarks. However, the older

5

and prettier she grew to be, the more dangerous these incidents became.

Chapter 3

Boots and Hecky Spinner are redneck losers. They have been in trouble with the law since they were twelve and fourteen years old. Now they're in their thirty's. They have been in and out of jail so many times that the experience has made them mean. They chew tobacco, drink moonshine because it's cheap and live in unwashed bodies. The tobacco and lousy personal hygiene have rotted their teeth.

They still live at home with their mother and father who are disgusted by them. Their parents put them out of the house one time and told them to find some place else to live. They refused to leave. They pitched a tent in the back yard and stayed there. After a week the yard looked and smelled like a pigsty. Since they were not allowed in the house, not even to go to the bathroom, they peed anywhere they stood when they had to go. However, their more solid waste products were deposited in one corner of the yard and that pile got higher and smellier every day. After a month, Henry and Mary Spinner couldn't take it any longer. The smell was invading the house. They let them move back in but they had to stay in the basement. They were not allowed upstairs. Mr. Spinner moved their beds down to the basement and they ate their dinner on the back porch. This is the only meal their mother cooked for them. It took Henry Spinner two weeks to clean up the back yard and neither boy helped.

There was an extra bathroom in the basement with a toilet and a sink. The toilet was used every day but the sink seldom had any water in it because they seldom washed.

Neither boy had a job because no one would hire them. The little money they managed to get, they stole. Sometimes their father would give them a little money just to get rid of them. The only time their parents had any peace was when Sheriff Lloyd locked them up.

One day after a very bad scene with his sons over money, Henry Spinner told his wife, "I swear Mary, sometimes I feel like lockin' those boys in the cellar and burnin' the house down with them in it. What have we done to deserve two boys like them?"

Mary is shocked. She had never heard her husband talk like that before. "Oh no Henry, don't say things like that! You're too fine a man to do somethin' so horrible. We didn't do anythin' wrong. Somethin' was the matter with them from birth. Somethin' went wrong in the womb. It wasn't anythin' we did. We're gonna have some peace soon. You know they can't stay out of jail for long. Maybe next time they'll do somethin' real bad to keep them there for a long time. I just hope no one gets hurt because of them."

Chapter 4

After his dance with the turtle, Caleb goes home for a few days. Now that he's retired and Lloyd Wall has the job as Sheriff, he's free to do anything he wants. At first all he wanted to do was sleep. He never got enough while he was working. He was tired all the time. Now he feels good. He's well rested but he doesn't have any thing to do. The house doesn't need any repairs. Lloyd has done a good job keeping the house and yard in good shape. Caleb doesn't like being idle. He tries to think of something to do that would take up some of the day's hours but since meeting Josette, he only thinks of her. He doesn't know her name or where she lives. He only knows she goes fishing at Blue Mountain Lake. He decides to go back to the lake and camp out for a few days, hoping she'll show up. She did say she was at the lake often. Caleb can't understand why he asked her no questions. He had been asking questions of everyone for thirty years as The Sheriff of Lylesville. Then he meets someone he would like to know everything about and all his training is forgotten. He sits in his living room remembering the details of meeting the only woman who has ever excited him. He wants to see her again. He smiles to himself as he replays in his mind the events of their first meeting. She has no southern accent so he assumes she isn't from the south.

"Enough of this day dreamin'. I'm goin' back to the lake." He springs into action and packs his car with enough camping, fishing gear and food for several days. It's been many years since he slept outside in a tent. He's a lot older now and just in case his bones rebel at this unfamiliar activity, he packs extra pillows and blankets. Caleb Carter is a happy man driving to Blue Mountain Lake.

When he gets there, it's still early morning. He goes to the same spot he first saw Josette and where he danced with the turtle. It was a funny scene and Caleb can't help smiling as he remembers it. "I sure hope she remembers this spot and returns." He plans to stay a few days so he takes his time setting up the tent. He has done this before but not in a long time. The day is beautiful and warm with just enough of a breeze to keep it from getting too hot. At last, the tent is up. Caleb is pleased as he checks his fishing gear and prepares to sit on the shore and fish. He brought his hip boots with him just in case he decides to wade in the water and fly fish later. Right now he only wants to relax and enjoy the day. He can see other people doing the same thing. He's on his back with his hands under his head and in the warmth of the sun, he drifts off to sleep. Then, a shadow falls across his body and cools the air. He opens his eyes to see Josette smiling down at him.

"Hi there, mind if I join you?"

Caleb jumps up with a big smile on his face. "I would love it. I was hopin' you would come. Here, let me help you with your gear. I'm glad to see you."

"I'm glad to see you too, Caleb. I have to work next week so I'm spending as much time here as I can this week. You haven't seen any more turtles have you?" They both laugh at this.

Caleb is thinking as he looks at Josette, What a vision of loveliness this woman is. I could wake up to that smile every day. He has never felt this way before and he's finding it hard not to put his arms around her and hug her close. Instead he asks, "What kind of work do you do?"

"I'm a substitute teacher. They call me sometimes when they need me. It's usually one or two days but this time they want me all week. So, this week I'm spending as much time as I can here before I have to go to work. I miss this place when I can't come."

Finally, Caleb has remembered to ask questions of this woman. He smiles as he asks, "Do you always come alone?"

"No, sometimes I bring my two grandsons but that's usually on the weekends. They're eight and ten years old and they are a handful."

"And what about their Grandfather does he come too?"

Josette laughs. "Caleb, are you trying to find out if I'm married?"

"It has entered my mind. A woman as beautiful as you, is usually married unless she lives in a town full of blind men. We men are fools when it comes to a beautiful woman. We usually don't let her stay single long."

Josette is smiling at his words. "Thank you for that compliment Caleb. I'm a widow and have been for a long time. I'm not interested in fools and there were a few of them around at one time. I had two girls to raise. I didn't have time for anything else, especially fools."

"Well, I'm a fool because as much as we talked since we met, I never asked you your name. Tell me your name so I can advance off the fool list."

Josette laughs hard at this, "I'm sorry Caleb. I never realized you didn't know my name. I thought I told you. I'm Josette Fuller and I'm pleased to meet you. I would never put you in the same category as a fool."

Caleb is happy. He gets up to check his line and help set hers. "There, the poles are all set for the afternoon. I sure hope this time a fish bites the line and that turtle is long gone. Have you ever cooked your catch out in the open as soon as you caught it?"

"No, I usually take it home and pay one of the boys in the neighborhood to clean it for me. I hate cleaning fish."

"Well you're in for a treat. As soon as we catch some fish, I'm gonna cook dinner for us. I've got all the fixins' in my tent. You watch the lines while I build a fire and get everythin' ready."

"You've got a tent? How long were you planning to stay here Caleb?"

Caleb looks at Josette for a few seconds then says, "Until you came Josette. Until you came."

She doesn't say anything as he walks toward the trees where the tent is. She can't see it from where she's sitting. Josette is thinking about Caleb's words. She knows he's flirting with her and she doesn't know what to do about it. She realizes he really doesn't know who she is. I've known him all my life and he doesn't know who I am. Does he think I'm a stranger and not from around here? He hasn't seen me since I was fifteen. He was already working in the Sheriff's department and I'm guessing he was about twenty-five at that time. I wonder if he remembers my father. They used to go hunting together. Daddy always said he was the fairest man he had ever met. Even though he was born and bred in the southern way of thinking, he never disrespected any one. Degrading someone just because of their color was just not his way. Caleb returns and interrupts her thoughts.

"Josette, I've got the fire goin'. Now as soon as you catch our dinner, I'll cook it. The coals are good and hot. They'll stay that way for a long time."

Josette laughs, "I think the fish are lazy and content to lay around in the sun like we are. Have you ever seen a more beautiful day?"

"As far as I'm concerned, the day is perfect. The beautiful lady is perfect and I like the way her name feels as it rolls off my tongue. It's a beautiful name. I've never heard it before."

"Oh I'm sure you have. You just don't remember right now."

Caleb is sitting on the ground next to Josette. He can't take his eyes off her. Just then his pole bounces and the line gets taunt. He grabs the pole and starts to reel in the line. "I think our dinner has arrived Josette. Are you hungry?"

Before she can answer, her pole bounces too. She was so excited watching Caleb bring in his catch, she forgot her line.

"Look Josette! You've got one too. Grab your pole quick."

For the next few minutes they're busy trying to land their catch. Caleb is laughing. "Look Josette, look at what I've got. Man oh man ain't he a beauty!" He holds up a Big Mouth Bass for her to see.

Josette is still struggling to reel her fish in. "Just a minute Caleb I've got one too. Glory be, will you look at that! This is the biggest fish I've ever caught."

"I haven't seen fish this big here either. They must weigh five or six pounds. Come on I'll clean them and show you how to cook them in a pit. The fire should be just right about now."

"In a pit? What in the world are you talking about?"

"Come on. I'll show you."

When they get to the tent she doesn't see a fire. "Where is the fire Caleb? I don't' see anything."

He walks past the tent to what looks like a pile of stones. He puts on a pair of gloves and lifts the top stone off. Red Hot coals are sitting in a hole in the ground with other stones around the rim of the hole. "See, now all I have to do is clean the fish, wrap them in foil with some seasonings and drop them on the fire. In about fifteen minutes, I'll throw some water on the fire, replace the cover stone for about ten minutes and then we can eat. The meat will melt in your mouth."

"Oh, I remember my father doing something like that with pork after he killed a hog. It took a long time. We couldn't eat the meat until the next day. Of course the pit was a lot bigger. I can't wait. This sounds so delicious."

"It is Josette. Why don't you pack up our gear while I fix dinner. Then we can sit and talk."

"Ok Caleb, I'll be right back." Josette runs to the lake to pack up. It's now getting late in the day. It will be dark soon. She talks to herself as she packs. "After we eat I'll have to leave but I sure don't want to. This man is too good to be true. I'm having such a wonderful time. He's so comfortable to be around. He's nothing like his reputation says he is. What will he say when I tell him who I am? Will everything change? I don't know but it won't change today. I'm not going to let anything spoil this perfect day."

Caleb is having similar thoughts. Where has this woman been all my life? She brings joy to my heart just being around her. I know I love this woman. I've only seen her once before but I know she's the one for me. Does it really work that way? I've been alone all my life and I've never been lonely. Now, not seein' her for one day and I know that sad feelin'. Ok Caleb, slow down don't scare her away. How can a woman that beautiful not have a man in her life? I sure hope she doesn't. I wonder where she's from. These thoughts are put aside for a while as Caleb prepares the fish and places it in the pit to cook.

Dinner is a big success. Caleb and Josette laugh and talk about everything except themselves.

Josette says, "Caleb, I was having such a good time, I forgot all about the time. I should have been gone, now it's dark."

"Please stay, Josette. Look, other people are still campin' out. Will anyone miss you if you get home late? I can always drive you home."

"What will I do with my Daddy's pick up if I let you drive me home? No Caleb no one will miss me. Now that my girls are married I live alone. I'm used to getting myself home."

"Before you go let me show you my castle." He takes her hand and leads her to the tent. "Look I've fixed you the finest bed in my castle."

13

On one side of the tent is a cot with pillows and blankets on it. The cot is only big enough for one. The floor of the tent is strewn with pillows on top of pillows, blankets and a sleeping bag.

"My goodness Caleb, I've never seen so many pillows before. You have every size and shape possible. This looks like a luxurious harem for many ladies. It's very nice but there's only one bed."

"That's because this room is for one lady only. My bed is the floor. I brought all these extra pillows because I'm not a young man any more and I don't know how these old bones will react to sleepin' on the ground. I haven't done that in a very long time."

"You're not that much older than I am. Remember, I told you I was a grandmother? Well, I'm a young grandmother and don't you forget it. I've never been invited to a castle before. Caleb, this is wonderful!"

Caleb inwardly is jumping with joy. There is a big smile on his face. "I was afraid you would say no. I was afraid this was gonna be a lonely night for me. I've never had that feelin' until you left the other day. All the way home I thought of nothin' but you. I felt somethin' was missin' inside me; somethin' vital that I need to live."

"Why Caleb, you hardly know me." Her voice is a whisper. "This is only the second time we've met."

"I know Josette, I know," is all he says as he stands there looking at her.

She breaks the silence first. "Well, if I'm going to spend the night in your castle we had better clean up out there first. We can't leave any garbage around for any wild critters to get. I've never spent the night here before and I don't know what animals are out at night but I do know, I don't want them around me."

Caleb smiles as he gathers up their plates and utensils. He puts everything they used in bags then in a portable garbage pail he brought with him. When he finishes, he says to Josette, "Don't worry sweetheart I've wrestled with the bears in these woods before. They are all afraid of me. They won't come near us."

They laugh and Josette says, "Come on Caleb it's getting late and cold. Let's go into the castle for the night. All that good food has me sleepy."

Caleb takes Josette's hand and kisses it. "You're safe here with me Josette, always remember that."

Josette settles down on the cot while Caleb tries to get comfortable on the floor. He's surprised the pillows are so comfortable. He may be comfortable but he can't sleep. His mind is on that beautiful woman sleeping just a few feet away.

"Caleb, are you awake?"

"Yes Josette, I'm awake."

"You don't like me very much do you?"

Caleb immediately sits up. "What! Oh Lord Josette, did I do somethin' wrong? Why did you say that? What did I do?" Caleb is visibly upset. He can't understand why she would say such a thing.

"Well, I was just wondering why you put me up here on this hard cold cot and you're down there on all those soft warm pillows."

Then she laughs and Caleb understands she's teasing him. "That's not fair girl, that's not fair." Caleb is relieved. His stomach had started to churn from fear and he broke out in a sweat. These emotions are new to him. He never felt any of them until he met her.

"Calm down Caleb. I'm teasing you. Can I come down there next to you? I'm cold up here." Then she says, "Caleb, I really mean next to you. I'm not ready for anything else. Can you exercise some restraint?"

He holds out his hand. "Come on sweetheart. There's plenty room down here and I can do or not do anythin' you want."

They get cozy on the pillows with her head on his chest and his arm around her. Then she snuggles closer and puts her arm across his abdomen. Caleb moans.

"What's the matter Caleb?"

"Nothin' Josette, I'm just exercisin' my restraint. It ain't easy." This remark breaks the serious mood and they laugh for several minutes. Sleep is lost for them as they talk and laugh until dawn.

"Caleb I want to tell you something. Please don't be offended by what I'm going to say, ok?"

"Ok sweetheart but there's no way you could offend me."

"You remind me of my late husband. You're very much like him. He was a big man too. He was gentle and caring and he never got my

15

jokes either. I would tease him just like I teased you a few minutes ago. After he died I was lost for many months. If I didn't have my two girls to take care of, I would probably be in the crazy house right now. I compared every man I met to him. They all came up short. I never dated in all those years. I missed him so much. Caleb, I'm glad I met you."

Caleb is quiet for a few minutes. He doesn't know what to say. Finally he says, "Thank you Josette. He sounds like a fine man to me. I'm not offended. I'm pleased."

After a few minutes they drift off to a peaceful sleep at dawn. They sleep until noon. Then the heat in the tent wakes them.

Chapter 5

The next morning, when Josette gets home from the lake her daughter Cathy is waiting for her. "Mommy, where have you been? I've been here all night. This is not like you. I was worried."

"Hush child, I've been taking care of myself for many years. I was up at the lake. You know I go there all the time. I'm going again on Saturday and I'll be taking the boys."

Cathy didn't hear a word her mother said. She continued her questions. "What's going on? Where did you sleep? What did you eat? You never stayed out all night before."

"Cathy, will you please stop. I can take care of myself. I met some nice people and we camped out all night. We cooked what we caught and stayed up all night talking. I have not been to sleep. Now go home! I'm going to bed! And tell your sister to stay home too. I don't want either of you waking me up."

"Ok Mommy," is all Cathy says but somehow she doesn't believe her mother. She worries all day until her sister Janet comes home from work.

Janet is surprised when she comes home to see Cathy sitting on her front porch. "What's the matter Cathy? Why are you here? Is Mommy all right? You look worried."

"I am worried Janet. Mommy's fine but I think she lied to me. You know Mommy never lies. She didn't come home last night. She stayed out all night! She never did that before. When I asked her where she was, she said she met some new friends at the lake and they were up all night talking. I think she lied to me. Why would she do that Janet, why?"

"I don't know Cathy but maybe it's none of our business. You know she goes to the lake all the time. You worry too much. Trust her. If it's something important she'll tell us when she's ready."

"Oh yeah? Suppose it's a man?"

"So what Cathy! All the time we were growing up didn't we want another Daddy? She wouldn't even look at another man. She had us. Now we're grown and gone. She lives by herself. Maybe she's lonely. Maybe it's time she got interested in someone. Let's wait and see. Now stop! Leave her alone!"

"You can say what you want but I'm gonna' watch her."

"Don't say, gonna', Cathy. You know Mommy doesn't like that."

"Don't change the subject Janet. Besides, I never say it around her. I'm grown now if I want to say it, I will! All the kids we grew up with made fun of us because of the way we talked. Why did we have to be so different?"

"Because Mommy was a teacher! That's why! Now stop! Go home Cathy! It's time to feed your husband and your boys."

"I'm going but you have been no help. I thought you would be concerned too."

"I am Cathy but Mommy will tell us when she's ready. She's entitled to her privacy. Let's wait."

Janet is annoyed with her sister because now she starts to worry too. "I wonder if she has met someone she likes or just new friends like she said. Maybe it's just that simple and Cathy is worrying unnecessarily. I've never known Mommy to lie." Janet is mumbling these words to herself as she prepares dinner for her husband.

Chapter 6

Meanwhile Josette is not sleeping. She's sitting in an upholstered chair in her bedroom thinking about Caleb. He acts like he doesn't know her but he must. He knew her father very well. They used to hunt together. It's been a long time since her father died and he did send her away to college when she was seventeen. The last time she saw Caleb, she was fifteen. Maybe she has changed too much and he truly doesn't recognize her. Joe Winters, Josette's father, thought he was sending her to a college that was set up years ago to teach the descendents of freed slaves. He thought it would be a good place for her. Joe Winters didn't know the school had changed. Though it was an excellent school, the student population had changed. It is now lily white. Not many colored families can afford the tuition. She wondered where her father got the money to pay her's. He never said.

No one knew she wasn't white until the end of her first year when her father came to take her home. After that, the next three years were hell but she Persevered. She refused to let the snide remarks and blatant racism get her down. She was determined to get her degree and not disappoint her father. She wanted to be a teacher. She realized how she and the other children she grew up with, were shortchanged by the school system in their town. They were given second hand books, many had missing pages, not enough pencils or paper and teachers who were not certified. These teachers did their best but there was a shortage of colored teachers in the south. There was also a shortage of white teachers that cared. Josette always resented the way the white teachers taught the colored girls. These girls were not encouraged to take classes that would get them into college. They were taught to be good housekeepers or good maids. One white teacher in particular made a point of telling the girls "When you get one of these good jobs, you must not steal. Above all else you must be honest." Did she think all colored people stole and had to be constantly bombarded with the commandment, "Thou shall not steal?" Did she think the only job a colored girl could do was being a maid or doing housework for white people? That particular teacher is the one who gave Josette the determination to be a good teacher. How dare she treat young girls that way?

Every time these thoughts come into her mind, after all the years that have passed, Josette still gets angry. She can feel the anger rising and tells herself, "Enough Josette, that part of your life is over. You've done your best. Every young girl you taught was encouraged. Go get your lesson plan for next week. Then go back to the lake to see if Caleb is still there. You know you want to see him again."

Chapter 7

As soon as school opens the next morning, Josette is there. She's anxious to get her lesson plans for the next week and be off to Blue Mountain Lake. Everyone was so busy at the school, that it took longer than expected. An hour later she's back home preparing to leave for the lake. She's excited at the thought of seeing Caleb again. Today, no thought of fishing is on her mind. She takes extra care with her appearance. She only plans to sit and talk with Caleb so she brought no fishing gear. She dresses in a long caramel colored skirt with walking boots to match. A red blouse and her thick wavy hair loose around her face hanging down her back completes her attire. A small amount of lipstick that picks up the color of her blouse is all the makeup she wears. She looks no-where near her fifty-one years. Josette Fuller is a beautiful woman.

She arrives at Blue Mountain Lake just before noon. She wonders if Caleb is still there. She goes directly to their spot. She thinks of the place they first met as their spot. The tent is there but Caleb isn't. She gets a few pillows from inside the tent and sits down to wait for him. She wonders where he is. She's been waiting about an hour when she hears someone running through the trees. She can't see who it is and it scares her. She quickly runs away from the tent and hides behind a large bush. She is afraid it might be the Spinner brothers and she doesn't want them to see her. She makes herself as small as possible under the bush and waits.

Suddenly, Caleb comes into the clearing calling her name. "Josette, Josette."

"I'm here Caleb."

"I saw your truck and came runnin'. I was afraid you would leave before I got back. I'm so glad to see you. I was hopin' you would come today. Saturday seemed so far away." Caleb is so happy and talking so fast, it takes him a few minutes to really see Josette. She is walking toward him smiling. She takes his breath away.

"Oh my God! Josette, Josette, you are the most beautiful human being I have ever seen." He takes her in his arms and whispers softly,

"I'm never gonna let you go girl, never, never, never." They stand there for a few minutes hugging each other. The top of Josette's head just fits under Caleb's chin. She has her head on his chest, her eyes closed and her arms around him.

Josette breaks the silence first and whispers, "Caleb I hope you really mean that."

Then Caleb realizes something. "Josette, why were you way over there when I called you? Were you hidin'?"

"Yes I was. I heard all this running and branches breaking. It made me nervous. I didn't know it was you."

"I'm sorry sweetheart. I saw your truck and I ran like hell to get here. I couldn't wait to see you. I didn't mean to scare you."

"It's all right. You're here now. I wanted to see you too. It's such a beautiful day, let's take a walk around the lake or did you want to fish?"

"No sweetheart, I'd rather walk with you. Later we'll go to the diner down the road and have dinner early. Then we can come back here and watch the sun go down on the water. I've watched it many times by myself. It's a beautiful sight. Now I have someone to share it with. Josette, I don't know how to say all the things I feel. This is so new to me but I do know, I never want you out of my life."

They walk slowly holding hands enjoying each other's company. Then Caleb says, "Do you know Reverend Remison Roberts from Lylesville?"

"Yes, I know him. My father introduced me to him when I was a little girl. I haven't seen him in many years."

"Well, I went to see him once when I was thinkin' about retirin'. I was concerned about it. I had a lot of questions and I needed some guidance. What would I do with all the free time I would soon have? Shall I stay in Lylesville or move some place else? Will the person who takes my place be a good sheriff and treat all people as fair as tried to do? I was worried about the Klan. I was only able to keep them in check because I knew them all and most of them were afraid of me. I saw to it that they stayed that way. With me gone as Sheriff would they begin to act ugly again? He gave me some good advice. He said, I had no control over my profession when I left it. The only thing I could do was pray that the next sheriff was a good man. Who that man would be is out of my hands. It took a long time for me to accept that. Then he said my personal life was another matter. He said God was all knowin' and merciful and he knew me. He would replace what I had with somethin' better. All I had to do was have faith that somethin' better was comin'. I believed him Josette. I believed him even though I've never been a religious man. I believed what he said about his God. Never in my wildest dreams could I know that somethin' better would be you. What a wonderful God he has."

Josette is surprised at Caleb's words. She stops walking and takes both his hands. "Caleb, God doesn't belong to any one group of people. He's everyone's God whether they believe in him or not. That's the beauty of God's love. Any one can go to him. No one is turned away. I know you've seen a lot of evil during your years as Sheriff but there's a lot of good in the world too. We can't let evil rob us of the joy of living. Life is our gift from God. I've seen and been the victim of evil too but my faith in God helped me through those bad times. I'm forever grateful to God for his help. I've been blessed Caleb and you are one of those blessings. I wasn't looking for you but now that you're here, I'm grateful."

Caleb is close to tears at her words. He hugs her close to him for a few minutes. They walk the rest of the way in silence. Caleb has his arm around her shoulders holding her close and she has her arm around his waist. As they walk and talk to other people fishing, time passes quickly and they arrive back at the tent late in the afternoon.

"Are you hungry Josette? I am. That exercise of walkin' made me hungry."

Josette laughs. "Exercise! That slow walk was not exercise. Yes I'm hungry too. I could eat something."

"Ok, let's go to the diner down the road. We'll eat there. The food is good." They run through the trees to Caleb's car holding hands. When they get to the diner, there's a sign out front with an arrow pointing to the rear. It says "coloreds only." Josette is brought back to reality with a jolt. Her day was so perfect she let herself forget about the ugly prejudice of the south. She has to think of something fast.

She dare not go in with Caleb. Someone may recognize her and she has not told him who she is yet.

"Caleb, do you mind if we not go in and be around a lot of people? How about getting our dinner and taking it back to the lake. I would like that."

"Good idea Josette, I'd like that too. I didn't want to share you with anyone else anyway." Caleb is smiling.

"You go get us something good. Surprise me and don't forget dessert."

"Ok sweetheart, I'll be right back."

Josette breathes a sigh of relief. "This is a wake up call. I had better tell him soon before anyone else does. When I bring the boys tomorrow, he'll know." Josette is nervous sitting in Caleb's car waiting for him. Several people walked by on their way into the diner but no one looked her way.

Caleb comes back with two large bags of food.

"My goodness Caleb. Did you buy out the place?"

Caleb winks at her, "Almost. I got enough just in case we work up an appetite and want a snack in the middle of the night."

Josette smiles. She was unsure how long she and Caleb would be together today. Now she knows. Poor Cathy is going to be upset again.

Caleb is busy setting up a folding table for dinner. He thought of everything. He brought a tablecloth, napkins, forks, knives, spoons and glasses. He even had a candle in the middle of the table. Of course it's a citronella candle to keep the mosquitoes away but it's a nice touch. He won't let her help.

"You just sit there and look beautiful. You're my guest."

Dinner was wonderful. Caleb had bought half the diner's menu and six desserts. He jokingly said to Josette, "This food will not go to waste. We'll work up an appetite and eat again later." It's the second time he said these words. Caleb is testing her to see her reaction but Josette just smiles and makes no comment. She insists on helping to clean up and put the uneaten food away. Caleb packs up the garbage and Josette brings the extra food into the tent. Working together makes the clean up go fast. In the tent, the cot and sleeping bag are gone but the floor is still a mass of pillows and blankets.

"Caleb your castle looks as comfortable as ever. Will it always be this way?"

"As long as you're in it, comfort and love will always be here but I have one question Josette. Are the restraints removed?"

She puts her arms around his waist, looks up and says, "What restraints are you talking about? I don't' see anything that could hold back a man like you. No Caleb, there are no restraints."

Caleb is smiling again. "Come on girl the sun is going down. Let's watch for a while and give our food time to digest." He takes a blanket with them and they sit at the lakeshore and watch the sun slowly slip below the horizon. Her left arm is around his back and her head is on his shoulder. He is hugging her close to him with his right arm. They share the beautiful sunset in the contentment of silence. When the sun is gone and the darkness brings the cool air, they leave the shore and go back to the tent. There is no need for conversation as they undress and get on the floor of pillows and under the blankets. Caleb is rejoicing in his heart. Finally the woman he has wanted so badly is in his arms.

Josette whispers, "Caleb, it's been a long time since a man has made love to me. Suppose I don't please you. Suppose I forgot."

"Josette, do you know how to swim?"

"Of course I do, Caleb"

"Well sweetheart, that's what it's like. You never forget. Once you start everythin' will come back to you. And if you don't please me, I'll drown you in the lake."

That starts the both of them laughing and several minutes pass before serious love making begins. Caleb and Josette are in love. Caleb is ecstatic and Josette is happy but fearful. She is afraid of losing this man she adores and says a quiet prayer. "Please God let him understand when I tell him who I am. I don't want to lose him."

They don't sleep much and Caleb was right. They work up a big appetite. They talk, eat the rest of the food and make love all night. They can't get enough of each other. When dawn creeps up on them, they moan in disappointment at seeing the light of day. They wanted this night to last forever.

Josette prepares to leave. "Caleb I'll be back sometime around noon with my grandsons. I promised to take them fishing. Will you still be here?"

"Oh yes. I'll be here. I know you have to go. You own my heart Josette. We belong together so hurry back."

Josette gets very serious and says, "Does that mean you wont drown me in the lake?" This starts them laughing all over again. He walks her to her pick up and is still smiling as she drives away.

Chapter 8

Josette arrives home in the middle of the morning. She is grateful Cathy isn't there to bombard her with more questions. Today, she is too happy to engage in a confrontation with her daughter. She expects Cathy to bring the boys around noon so she has plenty of time to change clothes. She doesn't want to explain to Cathy why she's dressed the way she is. How would she explain what she's wearing now? How could she tell her daughter she dressed just to please a man? She laughs to herself as she visualizes the look on Cathy's face if she had seen her mother last night in Caleb's arms. Josette's quiet laugh becomes louder as she says out loud, "Child you should have seen your Momma last night."

After a few minutes of hilarious laughter, more serious thoughts invade the moment. Cathy may never know her mother is in love again. Everything will depend on what happens today when Caleb sees her grandsons and she tells him she's Joe Winters daughter. If the situation goes terribly wrong, her girls will never know. However, if Caleb is the wonderful man he appears to be, then Josette is the one who will have a problem. How will she break the news to her daughters? How will they take the news that their mother is in love with a white man? How will everyone's life change because of it? What about her neighbors and friends? How will they take the news? She and Caleb are happy when they're together. Will that change? Josette doesn't know the answers to any of these questions. She only knows a big change is coming.

She hurries to get dressed before her daughter arrives. She finishes just as Cathy walks in with the boys and interrupts her thoughts. "Mommy, we're here. The boys are all ready to go."

"I'll be right down. I'm ready too." Josette runs down the stairs smiling at her grandsons. "Come on boys. Let's go fishing. Thanks for bringing them Cathy. We'll be back around suppertime and I'll drop them off. If we catch any fish, you can have them all. You know how I hate cleaning fish."

"Ok Mommy. Stevie and Timmy, you boys behave and bring home lots of fish. Have a good time. I'll see you later."

The boys wave good-bye to their mother. On the drive to the lake the boys are unusually quiet. Josette asks, "Is something wrong boys? You aren't talking. Don't you want to go fishing?"

Stevie speaks first. "Oh yes Grandma, we really want to go. Are our poles still in the back of the truck?"

"Yes they are. You know I wouldn't forget your poles. Now tell me what's wrong."

"It's Mommy. She said you were acting strange. Are you all right Grandma? She said to watch you and tell her everything you did."

"Did she say not to tell me?"

"No Ma'am."

"Well boys, don't you worry Grandma is fine. Your mother worries needlessly. I'll talk to her when we get back home. We're going to have fun just like we always do."

Josette is angry. Cathy had no business scaring the boys that way. She vows to take care of her daughter when she gets home. It takes a few minutes to get her anger under control but she does and the rest of the trip is as it should be. The boys are talking and having fun. When they get to the lake, the boys grab their poles and run ahead of Josette.

They yell, "Where should we set up Grandma?"

"Keep walking until I tell you to stop. I found a better spot a little farther around the lake. I'm bringing the bait."

Stevie and Timmy are skipping in the sand and every now and then they pick up a stone and throw it as far as they can into the water.

Caleb sees the boys before he sees Josette. Then he hears her voice calling them.

"Hey boys, someone is callin' you. Maybe you better wait."

They stop immediately, not sure what to do. They wait nervously until, Josette catches up with them but they never take their eyes off the big white man that stopped them.

Josette is out of breath from running. "Hi Caleb, it's getting harder to keep up with them. Boys I want you to meet Mr. Carter. He's a friend of Grandma's."

They say in unison, "Hello Mr. Carter."

"Caleb, don't just stand there help set the boy's lines so you and I can relax and talk while they fish."

"Sure Josette, come on boys I'll show you how to outsmart these dumb fish." Josette watches Caleb and her grandsons. They seem to be getting along fine. Finally the boys settle down to wait for a fish to bite.

Caleb comes and sits next to Josette. He smiles at her, takes her hand and kisses it. "I'm happy to see you again." He keeps her hand in his and says, "They look like they're having a good time. Do they always call you Grandma?"

"Yes Caleb, they do. I am their grandma."

Caleb looks at Josette with surprise. and says, "Do you wanna explain that to me."

"I do Caleb. That's why I brought them with me today. I never tried to trick you Caleb. I hope you believe that. I knew who you were as soon as I met you and you know me too. It took me a few minutes to realize you didn't recognize me."

"Wait a minute Josette. Are you tryin' to tell me you're not white?"

"That's exactly what I'm telling you Caleb. I should have told you sooner but I didn't want to spoil the easy way we had with each other. I was afraid."

"How do I know you? It's hard for me to believe I could have missed you."

"You haven't seen me since I was fifteen years old. You and my father were friends. Do you remember Joe Winters?"

"You mean to tell me you're that skinny little girl who used to hide behind Joe every time I came around? I always wondered why you were so afraid of me."

"Yes I'm that skinny little girl. I was afraid you would hurt my Daddy. Around that time a colored boy was lynched somewhere in the south. I didn't know where at that time but everyone was talking about it. I didn't know you and my Dad were friends."

"Yes I remember that incident very clearly. It happened in Mississippi. A fourteen-year-old boy from Chicago was the victim. That's when I vowed if I ever became Sheriff, nothin' like that would ever happen in my town. For thirty years it never did and I like to think I had a hand in preventin' such evil. But a year ago it did happen. That's when I finally decided I had enough. It wasn't a true lynchin' carried out by the Klan but it was made to look like one. Some one had a grudge against the victim. I never found out who it was." As Caleb said these words you could hear the sadness in his voice. "I remember you bein' a skinny little girl. You looked to be around twelve."

"I was fifteen. I grew a little after that. You didn't know it at the time but I had a big rock in my hand ready to hit you with if you tried to hurt my daddy. Everyone in Willow Park was afraid and angry because of that lynching in Mississippi. It was weeks before people settled down."

"You were protectin' your Daddy from me? Well I'm sure glad he was my friend" All of a sudden Caleb falls back on the ground laughing out loud. "I'm sorry Josette. I'm not laughin' at you. I'm rememberin' the diner the other day. That's why you didn't want to go in. I never caught on. I wanted to be with you so bad that what you said sounded like a good idea to me. You're a fast thinker Josette." Caleb gets quiet for a few minutes and Josette starts to worry. Then he gets serious. "Josette, your father was a fine man and I respected him. We got along fine. We stayed friends until the day he died and I missed him for a long time after that. Now, let me tell you somethin' girl. I don't care what color you are. You could be purple for all I care. I fell in love with you. As far as I'm concerned nothin' has changed."

Josette sits there with tears streaming down her face. The pressure is off and Caleb has lived up to her expectations.

He reaches over and hugs her. "Josette, You're not thinkin' about leavin' me are you?"

"No Caleb, but now we have some serious decisions to make. Our easy way of being together is going to get harder."

"Oh sure it is but not today. Today we're gonna have fun with these boys. There's no way I'm gonna let you go. So stop worryin'. We'll work somethin' out."

The rest of the day is a happy day. The boys caught lots of fish and Caleb showed them how to clean and wrap them so when they got home, the fish were ready to be cooked.

Josette's feeling of dread disappeared. Caleb and the boys got along fine. All the way home they talked about the big white man who helped them fish.

"Timmy, the talkative one, asks, "Grandma, can we tell Mommy about Mr. Carter?"

"Yes Timmy. You can tell your mother all about today. Wasn't it a beautiful day? Would you like to go fishing with Mr. Carter again?"

Stevie and Timmy both yell "yeah" at the same time. Then Stevie says, "Grandma, Mr. Carter said he could show us how to cook fish in the ground. Can he really do that?"

"He sure can. He showed me the other day. The fish was so good it melted in my mouth. We ate it all up. You'll see. If he said he would show you how, he will. Maybe next Saturday we can come again. Would you like that?"

They both yell, "Yeah, yeah and we can show him how to skip stones on the water." They are excited and looking forward to the next fishing trip.

Timmy's excitement infects Stevie. "Yeah and I'll pick the stones. You have to get the right ones. They have to be real flat or they won't skip good. Sometimes if you throw them just right they'll skip three times."

The boys and Josette are happy driving home. The boys are laughing and bouncing around in the truck while Josette smiles to herself as she remembers the pleasant day she and the boys spent with Caleb. She's especially happy that Caleb proved to be the wonderful man she expected him to be. She's glad she told him who she was early in their relationship before any one else did.

Chapter 9

Josette takes the boys home and helps them carry their catch in the house. They caught enough fish for everyone to have a good dinner. Cathy meets them at the door.

"Hi boys, did you have a good time?"

Timmy is very excited. "Yeah Mommy, we caught a lot of fish and Mr. Carter showed us how to clean them. It was fun and Grandma said we can go again next week. Can we Mommy, can we?"

"Sure you can Timmy but now you and your brother go wash up. I'll fix dinner and as soon as Daddy gets home we can eat."

Josette has left the house and is in her truck. Cathy comes out of the house running. "Mommy wait."

Josette didn't want to stop but she did. "What do you want Cathy? I have to get home."

"Who is Mr. Carter? The boys said he showed them how to clean the fish."

"He's some one we met at the lake. The boys had a good time fishing with him. Go feed your children and stop pumping them for information. They were upset when I picked them up. Why did you tell them to watch me? They thought something was wrong with me and they were worried. How dare you spy on me using your children! Don't you upset those boys like that again! They shouldn't be put in the position of worrying about their grandmother." Josette is very angry and can't keep it from showing on her face or in the tone of her voice.

Cathy starts to cry. She's not used to her mother yelling at her. "I'm sorry Mommy. I was worried that's all."

"Ok Cathy, I'll talk to you later. I'm going home. I smell like fish."

Cathy is upset but she won't leave well enough alone. She is positive her mother is hiding something and she is determined to find out what it is. When her husband gets home she has dinner ready. The family sits down to eat and Cathy says, "Stevie, why don't you and Timmy tell Daddy all about your fishing trip today?" There was a phoniness in her voice that fooled Timmy but not Stevie. Timmy is still excited about the fishing trip and bubbling over. He tells his father all about Mr. Carter helping them fish and showing them how to clean the fish. He tells about Mr. Carter's promise to show them how to cook the fish in the ground. "Grandma said we could go fishing next Saturday too. I hope Mr. Carter is there to show us how to cook the fish in the ground. Grandma said it makes the fish taste good."

Cathy's husband asks, "Who is Mr. Carter? Do we know him?"

Timmy is still talking. "Grandma said he's a friend of hers."

Stevie interrupts. "He's just someone we met at the lake, Dad. He was fishing too."

"You boys sound like you had a lot of fun with grandma. I think you can go with grandma next Saturday if you want to."

Conversation stops because the boys are busy eating. Cathy is not satisfied. "Does Mr. Carter have a first name?"

Stevie knows what his Mother is up to and quickly says, "You told us not to call grownups by their first name."

Timmy agrees. "Yeah Mommy, we only called him Mr. Carter, honest. Grandma called him Caleb but we didn't. We only said Mr. Carter."

Cathy has a mouthful of food and almost chokes when she hears Caleb Carter's name. "Caleb Carter is the Sheriff in Lylesville! Steven, did you hear what your son just said? Since when did Mommy and the Sheriff get to be friends? I can't believe this. I'm not letting my boys go fishing with no white Sheriff!"

Cathy's husband is alarmed at her words. "Calm down Cathy. Don't you think you're over reacting? Sheriff Carter retired last year. He's not the Sheriff anymore."

Stevie is getting upset because of his mother's reaction. "He's not a bad man Mommy. He was nice. He didn't even have a gun. Why can't we go with Grandma? He likes her and he likes us too. We had fun. It's not fair!"

Cathy is too upset to talk any more. She leaves the table and runs to her room.

Timmy has a frown on his face and says, "What's the matter with Mommy?"

Stevie yells at his brother. "You talk too much be quiet!"

Steven is not sure what's going on. "That's enough boys, your mother over reacted. You know how she gets sometimes. Everything will be fine. Don't worry about Saturday. If grandma comes to get you, you can go with her. Now finish your dinner then go out to play. I'll take care of Mommy."

When the boys get outside Timmy asks, "Why did you yell at me? What did I do?"

Stevie apologizes to his brother. He knows Timmy is just being a typical eight year old. "I'm sorry I yelled at you Timmy."

"It's ok but why is Mommy mad? Why did she yell. Is she mad at us? Did we do something wrong Stevie?"

"No we didn't. I don't know what's wrong with her. I guess we'll find out later. We'll ask Grandma on Saturday. Dad said we could go with her if we wanted to. We'll ask her then. Let's go play ball."

Meanwhile Cathy's husband goes in their bedroom to find Cathy crying. "What's going on? Why are you so upset? Your mother goes fishing at the lake all the time. This isn't the first time she took the boys either. She probably knows every one there. What's so different now?"

"I think Mommy is lying to me. She didn't come home the other night. That's not like her and all she would say was that she met some friends at the lake and they stayed up all night talking. I don't believe her. She wouldn't say who the friends were. Now I find out that friend may be Sheriff Caleb Carter! This can't be Steven, this can't be."

"Cathy, you are being silly. Why wouldn't your mother stay up all night talking to people she knows.? It sounds reasonable to me. I don't understand why you're carrying on so. You upset the boys and now I'm beginning to get upset too. Is there something you're not telling me?"

"You don't understand how things are here. You didn't grow up in the south. There's no way a white Sheriff can be a friend to a colored woman. You don't know what she went through when we were little." Cathy breaks down and cries harder. "Leave me alone Steven. I don't want to talk about this any more tonight."

"Ok, but I don't like the boys seeing you so upset. Get a hold of yourself. We'll talk later. Then you can explain to me what it is I don't understand."

That night Cathy tells her husband about the Spinner brothers. He doesn't know if he should laugh or be angry. He doesn't want his wife to see him smile so he hugs her tight and banks the fire of her anger. When she can no longer see him, he has a good laugh and his admiration for his wife takes a giant step.

Chapter 10

Josette is preparing for bed when the doorbell rings. She thinks it's one of her daughters and she doesn't want to talk to either one. She's tired. Today is Thursday and there's one more day to work. Since she retired, she's not used to working five days without a break. Whoever it is ringing her bell is persistent. "All right I'm coming! Wait a minute!" She opens the door with a frown on her face. Caleb is standing there smiling.

"Caleb, what are you doing here?"

"It's been a long week Josette. Can I come in?"

"Of course Caleb. Come in. How did you find out where I lived? Did I tell you?"

"Josette, I was a Sheriff for many years. I can find out anythin' I want. Are you angry with me?"

"No, I'm just surprised that's all. You're the last person I expected to see at my door. I'm happy to see you though. It has been a long week for me too."

Caleb sits on the couch and holds out his arms. "Come sit on my lap Josette. I have somethin' I want to ask you and I want to make sure you won't run away.

Josette laughs at Caleb's words. "Don't be silly Caleb. Why would I run away?"

She sits on his lap and they hug each other. The room is quiet for a few minutes. Both are content just to be close. There's no need for words.

Caleb breaks the silence first. "Josette, this emotion of lovin' a woman as much as I love you is new to me. I don't know how to handle it. When we're together I'm on a great high. The world's a wonderful place. Then, when we're apart and I don't see you nothin' seems right. Everythin' goes wrong. Is this the way love works? I never want to be away from you and I know that's not possible. Can you help me out here? What am I suppose to do? Am I just an old fool? I don't understand why I never loved anyone before."

"I don't know what to tell you Caleb. I only know I love you too. We have to give ourselves more time to understand what has happened to us. There's going to be some unpleasant times ahead just because of who we are and where we live. You must know that. Will our love for each other be strong enough? Are we strong enough not to let anyone spoil what we have? We're going to be tested Caleb. I've been tested before, have you? I know what's coming. You're used to dealing with lawbreakers. How will you deal with the supposedly good people who won't like you being with me? I'm talking about white southerners. People you know and see everyday. They won't like it Caleb. We have a lot of thinking to do. This love we have for each other may cause a lot of problems." Josette stops talking for a few minutes. Tears have started to fill her eyes and she has to stop in order to regain her composure. "I'm going to have the same problems but on a more personal level. I know I'll have a difficult time with my girls; Cathy more so than Janet. I believe they will come around though because they love me and when they see that you love me too, everything will be fine. My only concern is whether you can handle whatever happens until that time."

Josette is still sitting on Caleb's lap and he hugs her closer and softly says. "Josette, please marry me. I don't care about all of that. We'll work it out. Please say you'll marry me."

"Caleb! Are you serious? Have you thought this out? How can we do that?" Josette is shocked at Caleb's words. This is something she never thought of. Being in love and dating is one thing but marriage is something else. Most people, colored and white wink at a relationship such as theirs and not for the same reason. What they wink at is on the vulgar side. She tries to get up from Caleb's lap but he won't let her. He hugs her tighter to keep her there.

"What's to think about Josette? Isn't that what people usually do when they're in love?"

"Not people like us, Caleb. Not where we live. It's not accepted here. You know that. We have problems most lovers don't. Where would we live? I can't live in Lylesville and you can't live in Willow Park. I'm not saying no, Caleb. We need time to think things out so we won't be surprised when unpleasant events happen to us. We have to be prepared to handle anything together. How are we going to do that?"

"Josette Honey, we'll take it one step at a time. I've thought about where we would live. I've given my house to Lloyd. Although he doesn't know it yet. We'll buy another one somewhere on the edge of both communities."

Josette starts to laugh. "Caleb you're a dreamer. As soon as it's known you have a colored wife, how long do you think we'll be on the edge of either community? Our white neighbors are going to give us a hard time, especially me. They're going to be angry because now they'll think they have to move. They won't want to sell their homes and to make things worse they won't want to sell their homes to any one colored. White southerners are very unforgiving when their way of life is disrupted Caleb. You know that. You've seen neighborhoods change over the years. You've seen Willow Park change. Willow Park was once all white, now only colored people live here. If that factory up river had not polluted the river and killed most of the Willow Trees, it would still be an all white neighborhood. Are we strong enough to stand up to all that's going to come at us? What about the problems I'm going to have with my girls? I'm going to have a hard time when I tell them about us, especially with Cathy. She hates white men. Caleb, how am I going to tell her I'm in love with one?" Josette starts to cry. "I don't know what to do. You see it's starting already."

"Don't cry Josette. We'll work things out. We'll take it one step at a time and I'll wait. We don't have to rush. I just don't want to take a chance on losin' you." Caleb hugs her until she stops crying.

"I'm sorry Caleb. This could break us up. Outside pressure could take away the happiness we feel when we're together. We have to think about the consequences when our love becomes public knowledge. I think my girls will come around because they love me but what about other people? What about Lloyd and your friends?"

Caleb is just beginning to feel a little of the everyday pressure colored people live with all their lives. He doesn't like it. He tries to assure Josette everything will be all right. "Josette Honey, everybody don't have to accept us. There's plenty good people around us both colored and white. We'll be fine. It may take a little time for some folk but when they see how committed we are to each other things will change. I'm sure of it."

"I hope you're right Caleb, I hope you're right." She kisses him on the forehead and says, "Can I get up now? I love sitting on your lap but you're squeezing me too tight."

They both laugh as Caleb releases his tight hug. "I just wanted to make sure you didn't run away. One more question Josette. Does all these obstacles you see, mean you won't marry me?"

"No Caleb, I didn't mean to sound that way. I would love to be your wife but we have to do some heavy thinking about what we're going to face. We have to be sure we can take it. We have to be sure. We can't let anyone steal our joy. Some people are so mean and vicious they would spoil heaven if they were there."

"Josette Honey, let's not talk about this any more tonight. I want you to meet Lloyd so let's not meet at the lake Friday night. Come to my house. I'll cook dinner and I'll pick you up at six o'clock."

Josette is unsure and shakes her head no and says, "I don't know Caleb. Does Lloyd know who I am?"

"I don't think so. I want him to know you, Josette. Someday you're gonna be my wife. I took him in when his father died and he is like the son I never had. He should know the woman I love."

"I remember how his father died. You did a wonderful thing helping him the way you did. I'm a little nervous Caleb. Dont you think it's too soon to let other people know about us? I'll come to your house but let's not tell him we might get married just yet. We don't know ourselves. Let him think whatever he thinks. We'll tell everyone our personal plans when we make them. Ok?"

"Sure sweetheart it's ok with me. I'll pick you up on Friday at six. He kisses her, a long wanting kiss and says, "Restraint is hard Josette." They laugh at their very personal joke.

Caleb leaves Josette's house smiling and Josette goes back to her room humming a happy tune. She puts the problems she thinks are coming her way, into a little room at the back of her mind and slams the door. A door she knows will reopen all too soon.

Chapter 11

Caleb is at Josette's door six o'clock sharp on Friday. He had prepared the food early and was dressed before five-thirty. He was anxious to see Josette again but it was too early to pick her up. He forced himself to stay home until five-forty five. It was only a fifteen minute ride to her house. He checked the dining room table just to make sure he had not forgotten anything. It was set for three just in case Lloyd came home for dinner. Caleb hoped he would. He wanted the two people he loved the most to know each other. He also hoped Lloyd wouldn't stay too long after meeting Josette because he wanted to spend most of the night with only her. He had mixed emotions about this night and it made him a little nervous. In the dangerous job he held for over thirty years, he was never nervous about anything. He was confident about his ability to handle what ever came his way. He dealt with bigots, unscrupulous politicians, murderers, thieves and thugs. None ever made him nervous. Now a beautiful woman has come into his life and he's nervous about everything concerning her.

Caleb is a good cook and he's proud of the dinner he prepared. He made biscuits ready to pop in the oven as soon as he and Josette arrived back at the house. A big pot of Jambalaya and a pot of rice are on the stove all cooked and waiting to be eaten. Sweetened iced tea with lemon and mint is cold in the refrigerator. A tossed salad is in there too. Desert is Apple Brown Betty, still warm on the back of the stove. The hard sauce to put on the Betty is in a covered dish on the counter. It tastes better and melts easier at room temperature.

Caleb is a happy man preparing all that food. At last, it's five-thirty. He's smiling as he gets in his car and drives to Willow Park.

Josette is just as happy as Caleb is. She can't wait to see him and the afternoon hours creep by. In the excitement of choosing something pretty to wear she pulls every dress, skirt and blouse out of her closet and tries them on, mixing and matching every possible combination. She had forgotten the wonderful feeling of making herself pretty for someone special. She delights in twisting and turning in front of the full length mirror trying to see how she looks from the back. Finally she chooses a peach colored blouse, a skirt with tiny blue Forget Me Nots on a pale peach background. A narrow gold belt and beige sandals complete the outfit. The skirt stops at the bend of her knee and shows off a pair of shapely legs. Josette is pleased with the way she looks. Her dark brown hair is worn loose and frames her face. The peach colored blouse makes her complexion glow. She is beautiful and smiling when Caleb knocks on her door.

When Josette opens the door, Caleb is speechless. He stands there with his mouth open looking at her.

Josette laughs at the silly look on his face. "I'm ready Caleb. Are you going to stand there all night?

"My God Josette, how could I have missed you all these years? You're the prettiest woman I have ever seen. You're beautiful!"

"Thank you Caleb, for that lovely compliment." She reaches up and kisses him on his cheek. "Now, are we going to stand here all night or are we going to dinner? What did you cook?"

After a short struggle, Caleb gets his emotions under control and says, "It's a surprise but I promise, you'll like it. Josette, I'm an old man and you got me actin' like a lovesick kid. I hope I can keep my eyes on the road. I'm havin a hard time takin' them off you."

They laugh and Josette says, "That's ok Caleb. I feel like a schoolgirl on her first date with a boy she's had a crush on for a long time. I had forgotten what fun it is to dress for someone you care for. It's been a long time since I did that but the expression on your face told me I did it right. Everything about us has been a long time coming and worth every minute."

They hold hands all the way to Caleb's house with a contented silence between them. Caleb is thinking, I must have done something right in my life to be rewarded with a woman like Josette. I'm one happy man.

Josette is praying. Please God don't let anyone spoil our plans for the future. You've sent another wonderful man to me. Please help me keep him.

Caleb pulls into his driveway and doesn't see Lloyd's car. "It looks like Lloyd hasn't come home yet. I want you to meet him Josette. He had a hard time as a kid but now he's a fine young man.

He's been livin' with me for twelve years now. I like havin' him around. I'm sure he'll be home sometime tonight. Let's go in the house and you sit at the kitchen table while I shove the biscuits in the oven. In ten minutes we can eat." They get out of the car and walk to the house holding hands. Just before they get to the door Caleb leans over and whispers in Josette's ear. "I'll make a good husband Josette. I know how to cook."

Josette puts her arm around his waist as they walk to the kitchen. "Caleb I've laughed more since I met you than I have in fifteen years. Thank you. Something smells mighty good. What did you cook? Whatever it is, it's making me hungry."

"Come look in this pot and tell me what you see." Then he changes his mind. "No wait. Close your eyes and see if you can guess by what you smell."

"Oh my, this smells so good." She leans over the pot with her eyes closed. "I smell seafood, hot peppers, Cajun spices and Oh my goodness! You made Jambalaya. What a treat! Are those biscuits done yet? I can't wait!"

"They sure are. You get the salad and the iced tea out of the fridge and we can eat.

Dinner was another delightful event in their relationship. They sit next to each other at the kitchen table instead of eating in the dining room where Caleb had set a beautiful table. They were having so much fun in the kitchen that Josette suggested they stay there. "Caleb why don't we eat here? It's cozier and if we want seconds, no one has to get up and go in the kitchen. We can put every thing on this table and if we want more all we have to do is reach for it. The dining room table is so beautiful let's not mess it up." That table stayed set and looking beautiful for two months. Lloyd is the one who put everything away. He thought he was doing Caleb a favor. He wasn't. Caleb was disappointed. He liked looking at the table. It brought a smile to his face remembering the Jambalaya he and Josette shared. He assumed Lloyd was doing something to please him so he said nothing.

Lloyd came home in the middle of the meal. He smelled the food as soon as he came in the door. When he walked into the dining room and saw the table set, He calls out to Caleb. "Hey Caleb what's goin' on? Are we havin' company?" He stops short at the kitchen door when he sees Josette.

Caleb speaks up immediately. "Hey Lloyd. Yeah, we got company. I want you to meet Josette. Josette, this is Lloyd. He took over my job as Sheriff when I retired. Close your mouth Lloyd you're starin'." That remark started the three of them laughing.

Josette extends her hand, "I'm pleased to meet you Lloyd. Caleb always says good things about you."

"I'm pleased to meet you too Miss Josette. Excuse me for starin'. I've been livin' with this man for twelve years and you are the first lady to come in this house. You must be somethin' special. You're also the prettiest woman I've ever seen. Has Caleb been hidin' you someplace?" He hasn't said one word about you."

Josette laughs, "We just met Lloyd. Sit down and join us. Caleb cooked enough to feed the whole town."

"I don't wanna intrude but I can't resist Caleb's Jambalaya. I'll just stay for a bit then leave you two alone."

The three of them talked and laughed for an hour. Caleb was happy Lloyd and Josette got along so well. He wasn't sure how Lloyd felt about women after Ellie May's betrayal. She was the only woman Lloyd ever loved.

Finally Lloyd gets up. "I gotta go Caleb. Leave the dishes. You two enjoy yourselves. I'll clean up when I get back. Miss Josette this house will never be the same. Please keep comin' back."

"I will Lloyd, if Caleb invites me."

"He better Miss Josette, he better. I'll see you later Caleb."

Caleb takes Josette's hand and kisses it. "Thank you sweetheart for bringin' laughter to my house. There wasn't much in the past. Lloyd has been through some bad times in his life. It's good to see him laugh so much. I don't think he'll mind if we get married. He seems to like you a lot."

"I like him too Caleb. He has sad eyes though. Did you see the shocked look on his face when he saw me sitting here? Is it true what he said about no women being in your house?

"Yeah it's true. Lloyd never brought a girl home either He only loved one girl that I know of. They were friends since they were children. Her father kept them apart but they still managed to see each other. Her father didn't like Lloyd and called him white trash. Then about two years ago, she betrayed him with another man. I don't think he's gotten over it yet. He will though. He's a strong man."

Josette is not so sure. She saw something more than sadness in his eyes. She likes Lloyd but now she feels sorry for him. She keeps this to herself. She knows how Caleb feels about Lloyd and she doesn't want to worry him.

Chapter 12

Caleb gets up from the table. "Come on Sweetheart, Lloyd said he would do the dishes. So, why don't you and I go sit on the front porch for a while."

"I don't like leaving a messy kitchen Caleb."

"Don't worry. It's ok. Lloyd and I have an agreement. I cook and he cleans up. It's been workin' for a long time. Let's not change it he might get spoiled."

Josette laughs and says, "That's fine with me. I would like to sit on the porch. There's something peaceful about sitting outside on a warm summer night."

They walk to the front porch holding hands.

Caleb says, "I wont turn on the light. We don't need it. There's a full moon and we don't want to share the porch with a lot of suicidal bugs."

"Oh Caleb, you have one of those old porch swings. My Daddy had one when I was a little girl. I've always wanted one. Where did you get it?"

"Do you know Roxie's Used Furniture store on Main Street? I got it from there but not from her. Old man Butler was bringin' a truckload of furniture to sell her and I saw it on the truck. I bought it from him before she saw it. Boy, was she mad! She called me a crook. She overcharges folks for that junk she has in her store and she calls me a crook. I paid him ten dollars for it and gave him an extra ten to deliver it to my house and put it on the porch. That was about eight years ago. It was a little beat up but Lloyd cleaned and painted it as a surprise for my birthday."

"Does it squeak when it rocks?"

"Not any more. Lloyd oiled it and removed the squeak."

"That's too bad Caleb. He took all the flavor out of it. I used to rock back and forth on my Daddy's porch swing just to hear it squeak. The harder I rocked the louder that squeak got. I did that when I was happy. It made me laugh. I thought the swing was laughing with me. When I was feeling sad, I would sit and slowly rock back and forth.

Then, the squeak would be soft and comforting. I never knew what happened to that old swing."

They sit together on the swing and slowly rock back and forth. Josette has her head on Caleb's shoulder. His arm is around her holding her close. They share a peaceful silence.

After a while Caleb says, "When we get married, we can take this swing with us and put it on our porch. Maybe after a few years it will start to squeak again."

Chapter 13

Lloyd came home around midnight. The house was dark. He assumed Caleb had taken Josette home until he heard soft laughter coming from his room. He smiled as he walked quietly past the bedroom door.

Earlier that evening Caleb had asked Josette to stay the night and was happy when she said yes. They didn't sleep much. After making love they rested in each other's arms and quietly talked.

Caleb asked Josette what happened to Cathy to cause her to hate white men so much.

"Well, it's a sad and funny story and I wish it had never happened. It's sad because of the way it affected Cathy but she was one feisty little girl. I was very proud of her that awful day. I used to take the girls with me everywhere I went. Their father had died two years earlier and I didn't want them out of my sight. Janet was twelve and Cathy was ten. We shopped for food and clothes every Saturday. It was a treat the girls looked forward to and I did too. We had so much fun together. The Spinner brothers stopped all that and Cathy never got over it.

They were teenagers then and had been in trouble with the law several times. It seems whenever they got in trouble with the law it was always in Willow Park. Maybe if they had acted up in Lylesville where you were, their punishment would have been more severe and maybe they wouldn't be so rotten now.

One Saturday we were on our way home with our groceries. I had bought each girl a new dress for church. Just as we got in front of The Bucket, we saw the Spinner brothers on the sidewalk in front of us. Do you know that bar they call The Bucket?

"Yeah I know it. I've been there a few times looking for some bad guys."

"Well, Big Sam owns it now. He used to work there as a bouncer. He's a tough man. I guess one has to be in that kind of job. He's married and owns a house in Willow Park. Do you know what? He and his wife come to church every Sunday. Everyone likes Big Sam. I guess business was slow that Saturday afternoon because Big Sam was looking out the window of the bar when the Spinner Brothers stopped in front of us and wouldn't let us by. Hecky, the older one said, "Looka here Boots, three pretty dinges. I like the Momma. Which one you like?"

"I was scared for my girls. I didn't know what to do. Hecky grabbed me and started squeezing my breasts. Boots went after Janet but she was too fast for him. She ran around me several times while he chased her. Just before he caught her she stopped short and ducked down. Boots wasn't expecting that and he tripped over her and fell head over heels on the ground. He hit His head and was bleeding profusely. He sat there in a daze looking at the blood on his hands. Cathy was jumping up and down crying and all of a sudden she kicked Hecky on the leg. I guess she was trying to make him let me go and he did but he hit her. Janet jumped on his back and some how Cathy grabbed Hecky's thumb and bit him. She had his whole thumb in her mouth and wouldn't let go. I managed to get Janet off him but Cathy wouldn't let go. He was swinging her around yelling his head off. He almost lost that thumb. Big Sam is the one who saved it for him. He was the only one who could make Cathy let go. When she did, she was spitting blood and crying. I was scared. I thought he had hurt her when he hit her. I thought it was her blood but it wasn't. Our groceries were all over the ground. While I was sitting on the ground trying to calm my girls down, Big Sam had come out of the bar and grabbed both boys by their arms and dragged them over to the side of the building where no one could see them. I found out later what he said to them. His wife told me. They were scared when he let them go."

All of a sudden Caleb falls back on the pillow laughing. "Are you tellin' me, that little girl almost bit his thumb off? I'm sorry I'm laughin' so hard sweetheart but the way you tell it, I can see him yellin' like a stuck pig. It's funny now but I'm sure it wasn't funny then. What did Big Sam say?"

"Well, while he was dragging them by their arms, they were calling him some very nasty names. They even threatened to come back some night and burn down his bar. He didn't want the girls to hear what he said to those boys, that's why he dragged them away. He told them I was his woman and if they ever bothered me or my girls again he would kill them. He said he would wait until they were drunk and catch them in the dark and kill them and no one would ever know who did it. I think that's what scared them because they're always drunk.

Big Sam is a powerful man and he had no trouble holding on to them while he threatened them. When he let them go, they ran off like a dog with his tail between his legs.

That was a strange day Caleb. Usually that street is busy with people coming and going either home, to the bar or shopping. That day, there was no one around and the bar was empty. No one saw what happened. The girls and I never told anybody, but that experience made Cathy an angry woman. It breaks my heart because I could never make her believe all white people were not like the Spinner boys. After that I stopped taking the girls shopping with me. I was afraid for them. Cathy became very bitter. She blamed the Spinners for spoiling our happy shopping days. I understood the way Cathy felt but I couldn't take a chance on those drunks hurting my girls. Those rotten boys stole some of the joy from our lives." Tears filled Josette's eyes as she said these last words. "The next Sunday, I caught Big Sam's eyes in church and whispered, thank you."

After that day the Spinner brothers stayed away from the vicinity of The Bucket. They didn't want to run into Big Sam but they continued to harass Josette whenever they saw her. They didn't see her often. Josette was always on the alert and most times she saw them first and changed direction before they saw her. Those were difficult years for Josette and she still feels a burning anger when she thinks about that time in her life.

Caleb doesn't know what to say. He feels anger too. He hugs her close to him. The room is quiet for a few minutes then he tells Josette, "I can't help what happened in the past sweetheart but I can promise you this. Those boys had better not come near you ever again."

"That was a long time ago Caleb. I've managed to avoid them over the years. They're not worth talking about any more. I promised my grandsons I would take them fishing again tomorrow. Are you free to join us?"

"I sure am. Suppose I come to your house and pick you and the boys up; no need to take your truck and my car."

Chapter 14

Cathy and the boys arrive at Josette's house before Caleb does. The boys are excited but try to keep their excitement down in front of their mother. Stevie had told Timmy to be cool and not to act too excited until after their mother left. Stevie is only ten but a little too wise for his age. He immediately picked up on his mother's dislike for Mr. Carter. He doesn't understand why she feels the way she does, so he tries to keep his younger brother's feelings for Mr. Carter in check when his mother is around. It isn't easy. He tells himself, "Timmy is just a little kid. He likes everybody."

Josette hears them on the porch and comes down to meet them. "Hi boys, are you ready to catch all the fish in Blue Mountain Lake?"

Timmy can't keep his excitement in check. "Yeah Grandma, can we cook the fish too? Me and Stevie will clean them. We ran all the way over here. We didn't want to be late when Mr. Carter came."

Stevie punches his brother in the arm and whispers, "Shut up!"

"Ouch! Mommy, Stevie hit me." When he sees the look on his mother's face; he shuts up immediately.

Cathy spins around and glares at her mother but before she can say anything. Josette holds up her hand and points her finger as if to say, "Keep your mouth shut girl. Don't you dare say one word." Cathy knows what this gesture means and the look on her mother's face scares her. She has seen it a few times as a child. This is not the time to confront her. She leaves her mother's house running. Her face is wet with tears and she's shaking with anger.

Caleb is just pulling into the driveway when Cathy passes his car running. She doesn't stop or look his way. By the time she gets home, she is in an uncontrollable rage. It's a good thing her husband isn't home or he would have been the object of her anger.

Meanwhile Josette and the boys are having a good time. They just finished transferring their fishing gear from Josette's truck to the trunk of Caleb's car. They all pile in his car to leave for the lake when Josette remembers the bait.

"Wait Caleb, we forgot to dig worms for bait."

"No need Josette, I stopped at the bait store. There's plenty in the trunk. I also stopped by the food store and got some snacks for us to munch on while the boys are fishin'. Hey boys, are you gonna catch a lot of fish for dinner?"

Timmy is still excited; nothing can keep an eight-year-old down. "Yeah Mr. Carter, I'm gonna catch the most and the biggest fish in that lake." Everybody laughs except Stevie. He's a worrier and right now he's worried about his mother. He didn't like the way she looked when she left grandma's house.

By the time they arrive at the lake, Stevie's mood has changed for the better. He's looking forward to fishing. They go to their favorite place. This spot is special to Josette and Caleb. The boys and Caleb are busy setting the poles while Josette sits on the bank watching them with a smile on her face. Troubling thoughts keep trying to invade her peace but she backs them off and slowly they recede to wait for another time when she's not so happy. Today, she, Caleb and her grandsons are having a good time. Everybody is happy until late afternoon when trouble comes to the lake.

Stevie sees them first. He and Timmy had taken a break from fishing and were skipping stones across the lake when he hears the Spinner brothers. They drop their stones and run calling, "Grandma, Grandma they're here. It's the Spinners, Grandma! It's the Spinners, they're here!" The boys are out of breath from running and both are close to tears. They know these men call their Grandmother bad names and they're afraid. They run to her side.

Josette is taken by surprise and berates herself for letting her guard down. She's close to tears too. She's afraid she has put her grandsons in danger. The memory of the last time the Spinners caught her and her daughters comes flying back and hits her in her gut. Her hands are shaking as she says, "It's all right boys. Run to the car and lock yourselves in. I'll be right there."

Josette hears the Spinners before she sees them. She starts to pack up to leave. "Caleb, we have to go."

Caleb is confused. Everything was so peaceful. They were enjoying the day and all of a sudden she wants to go. "What's the matter Josette? Have I done somethin' wrong? We're havin' such a good time, what's goin' on?"

"It's not you Caleb. I just have to go."

The look on her face has him alarmed. She's looking past him. Caleb turns around to see what she is looking at. The Spinner brothers are coming towards them. Now he understands and a cold anger takes over his body as he prepares to confront these two men who have ruined his peaceful day. "Don't be afraid of them Sweetheart. I told you I wouldn't let them bother you again. Don't you remember? I meant it Josette. I meant it."

"Oh Caleb, you don't understand. They're crazy mean. You don't know what they're capable of. It would be better if they didn't see me.

Stevie speaks up. "She's right Mr. Carter. Every time they see Grandma, they say bad things and call her bad names."

It's too late! The Spinners have seen Josette and they're yelling "Hey pretty Josette. We got somethin' sweet for you. Wait up, we're comin'." They're waving their arms and staggering. They appear to be drunk. These two look bad when they're sober. When they're drunk they're down right ugly.

Caleb calmly says, "Don't worry Josette. I'll take care of this. If you want to go, go on but you don't have to."

"Oh be careful Caleb, they're mean and sneaky. Maybe we should both go and avoid trouble." Josette says these words with anguish in her heart. She's afraid for herself, Caleb and her grandsons.

"Don't worry sweetheart, I've been handlin' this kind of trouble for thirty years. These two will soon find out how I do it."

Josette would like to leave but Caleb's attitude fascinates and excites her. She sits on the bank and watches. The boys didn't go very far. They came back and sat behind their Grandmother. She knew they were there. They were very quiet and each one had a big rock in his hand. The three of them watch Caleb as he stands there with his legs spread apart and his arms folded across his chest. Josette stares at Caleb's arms bulging with muscles. They appear to be hard as rocks. She felt his strength when he hugged her but she didn't realize he was so powerfully built. In the presence of apparent danger, she has the urge to run her hands over his arms and feel his strength. She whispers to herself, "That is one fine specimen of a man."

Caleb remains calm as he says, "Ok boys stop right there. We're tryin' to fish in peace and we don't want trouble."

"We don't want trouble neither Mister. We come to see Josette. She's the prettiest dinge we ever saw. We just wanna talk to her."

"I'm not gonna let you do that, so why don't you go on about your business and avoid trouble you can't handle."

Hecky is doing all the talking. Boots is standing there grinning and showing all of his rotten teeth. "Just who the hell are you mister? You don't own this here lake. We got as much right to fish here as you. Is Josette your woman? Are you a nigger lover?"

Now, Caleb is really angry but he remains calm as he says, "I'll tell you what I am, you piece of human garbage! I'm a white ass kicker. Now move on before I show you how I do that."

Boots is no longer grinning; he's nervous. "Come on Hecky, let's go. We can git her later."

"Hell no! We ain't goin'. He can't take both of us. Do you think you can Mister?"

Caleb smiles and says, "Without a doubt boys, without a doubt."

The Spinners hesitate as Caleb's words sink in.

Josette can see Caleb's muscles tighten in his arms and legs as they expand and get ready for action. All of a sudden the Spinner brothers rush Caleb. Josette lets out a yell. Caleb doesn't move but when they get close, his arms shoot out so fast and hard the Spinners don't see what's coming as he hits each one on the side of his head. Their knees buckle and Caleb stands there and watches as they fall at his feet. Then he drags them by their collars over to a small tree and props them up against it. He removes their belts and buckles them around their necks to the tree. The belts just fit with a little room to breathe. When they come to, they should be able to free themselves if they don't struggle too much and choke to death.

Caleb hugs Josette close and says, "Come on Sweetheart, our peaceful day of fishin' is over. Come on boys let's go."

Josette is in awe of Caleb's lightning fast moves. "My goodness Caleb, where did you learn to fight like that? It wasn't even a fight. You ended it before it got started."

"I've had thirty years of dealin' with garbage like that. You learn to be quick and not give fools like that the upper hand."

"Thank you Caleb. I was always able to get out of their way before. I'm glad you were here." She reaches up, takes his face in both hands, and kisses him on the lips.

Caleb smiles. "I love the way you say thank you, Josette. Do you wanna say it again?"

"I will Caleb but at another time. Right now I want to leave here before they wake up." Then she remembers the boys. "Stevie, Timmy are you all right?"

Her grandsons are excited and laughing. Stevie says, "We're fine Grandma. Maybe now those two won't bother you again. Mr. Carter, you sure can fight!"

Timmy is laughing too. "I bet they won't wake up till tomorrow. You hit them real hard Mr. Carter. I'm sure glad you did. I got scared when they ran at you. I bet they won't mess with you again!"

Josette hurries to leave. "Come on boys let's get our gear and get out of here."

Caleb and the boys work together and get everything packed quickly. The boys run ahead laughing. When they get a good distance in front of Josette and Caleb, Stevie says, "Timmy, Mr. Carter kicked ass!" This makes them laugh. On the ride home in the back of the car, they whisper to each other again and again, "Mr. Carter kicked ass." They roll around on the seat laughing harder each time they say these words. They think their Grandmother can't hear them but she does. The truth is, she's laughing too but she's trying very hard to hold it in. She doesn't want to set a bad example in front of the boys. Finally, she can hold it no longer and laughs out loud. Her tension is released and she and Caleb join the boys laughing. They are still laughing when they reach the boy's home.

Boots wakes up first. He jerks upright and feels the belt tighten around his neck. He thinks someone is choking him. He panics and thrashes around kicking and screaming. There isn't much room between the belt and his neck and all that kicking and screaming causes him to pass out from lack of air. His brother Hecky is a bit smarter. He wakes up a little calmer. He has a headache and puts his hands to the sides of his head before he realizes something is around his neck. He doesn't panic like his brother did. He feels around his neck and finds the buckle and frees himself. Then he gently removes the belt from his brother's neck. He can see bruises on his brother's neck so he doesn't want to alarm him. Hecky shakes Boots to wake him. Boots wakes up screaming and swinging. One blow catches Hecky between the eyes and for the next three weeks Hecky has two black eyes. He grabs his brother's hands and yells at him. "Cut it out man, cut it out! It's ok now; he's gone, calm down."

Boots starts to cry. "He was chokin' me Hecky! He was chokin' me! What did he hit me with Hecky? My head hurts."

"It's ok Boots. He's gone. Come on get up and stop that blubberin'. You sound like a baby. Let's go home and think of a way to get even with Sheriff Caleb Carter."

"I can't help it. I was scared. He ain't the sheriff. That ole mean Lloyd Wall is Sheriff."

"No, he ain't now but he was. Didn't you hear that gal call him Caleb? That was Caleb Carter from over in Lylesville. I didn't recognize him cause he didn't have a uniform on. Come on let's go home and find a way to get even with him and that gal."

"Hecky, I ain't messin' with that feller no more. Let's leave him alone. He hits too hard. I don't want him hittin' me again. He hit me with his fist. I know he did."

"No he didn't! Nobody got hands that hard. He hit us with a rock and I'm gonna find a way to get even."

When these two try to get up, they can't. In addition to their heads hurting from Caleb's punch, they also have a bad hangover. Trying to stand makes them dizzy so they sit for a while longer. Hecky gets himself together first.

"Come on Boots let's go. I need a drink to clear my head." He helps his brother up and they stagger away from the lake holding each other up. They're a sad and smelly sight.

Not being fast thinkers or good planners, it takes three months for these two to cause trouble for Josette and Caleb. To Hecky's surprise it's Boots who comes up with the idea. However, that idea caused them to get a jailhouse whipping and Hecky almost dies.

Chapter 15

Josette has a hard time sleeping that night. She can't get Caleb off her mind. She keeps seeing his hard rock body standing in front of her. He is the only man that has excited her since her husband died many years ago. Caleb reminds her of him. He was a powerfully built man also and as long as he was alive he was her protector. Now another protector has come into her life. She wonders if he will stay when the south stomps on their relationship. Will he be as strong mentally as he is physically? "Oh, I hope so. I'll wait and see as time passes. I sure do like that man." Josette says these words to herself just before she drifts off to sleep and dreams of being in Caleb Carter's arms.

Caleb isn't doing any better. He keeps reliving her kiss. Her lips were soft and warm on his. He wanted her to kiss him again but the boys were there. That vivid memory has erased the Spinner Brothers from his mind completely.

He can't wait to see her again. All the years he has been alone has been ok with him. He has not been lonely and he never met anyone he wanted to be with for any length of time. His job kept him too busy to socialize. Many of the local single women tried to get him interested but it only lasted for a short time. After a while they gave up on him and moved on to more promising prospects. Caleb was relieved when this happened. He was tired of being polite.

His life settled down to a comfortable routine. Then he retired, met Josette, and now nothing is routine or comfortable anymore.

Two images keep appearing in his mind; the sight of her hair hanging down her back as she sat on the lakeshore singing softly and her soft lips on his when she said thank you.

All night they dreamed and thought about each other.

Chapter 16

Caleb Carter is the only child of Merlee and Larry Carter. Merlee was the typical Southern Belle without the attitude of entitlement or the pretense of superiority. She had a wholesome down to earth air about her. She was tall, slender and flirty. Anyone meeting her liked her immediately. Her family was from Willow Park; an affluent white community on the Saw Mill River. They left Willow Park when the river was polluted by the saw mill and most of the Willow Trees died. They moved to Lylesville and that's where Merlee met Larry Carter. She liked him immediately and he was smitten. It took him a while to convince her to marry him. Finally after much begging and pleading on his knees, she said yes. They had a good marriage and she always teased him about his begging. He always said, "A man's gotta do what a man's gotta do." This was their private joke and they laughed over it often.

Larry Carter was a gentle giant standing six feet five inches tall. He was quick to smile with a pleasant personality and always willing to lend a helping hand to anyone in need. He didn't have to know you to help you.

They were married for ten years when Caleb was born. They thought they would be childless and then, Caleb came into their lives and they spoiled and adored him. He was their blessing. He was a happy child but he didn't have many friends. He refused to join the other kids when they wanted to torment some of the colored kids that lived on the other side of the tracks. His mother told him this was a wrong thing to do. No one had the right to be unkind. The white kids who could have been his friends didn't want to play with him because they said he thought he was better than any one else because his ass was so far above the ground. Caleb was a good twelve inches taller than all of them by the time he was thirteen.

One Saturday, Caleb was fishing in the creek and as usual he's alone. He hears a crowd of people coming his way. They're laughing, drinking and shooting guns in the air. He hides in the tall grass to watch. Their guns scare him. They pass close to where he's hiding and stop beneath a large Cotton Wood Tree. Caleb is thirteen and he is about to see a lynching. It scares him so much that he wets his pants and throws up. He doesn't see the victim at first. He didn't know what all the revelry was about. All of a sudden a colored man flies up out of the middle of the crowd with a noose around his neck. Three men are pulling on a rope thrown over a lower branch of the tree. They hoist him up as far as they can while his legs kick, his eyes bulge and roll back in his head. It only takes a few minutes for him to die but a lot longer for him to stop moving while the crowd cheers. They leave him hanging there.

Caleb thought the man would never stop swaying. When the crowd leaves, Caleb runs home to get his father. His father is furious. His mother hugs him and cries with him. This act of compassion helps him over the fear that has his body shaking. Later that fear is replaced by an anger that stays with him into his adult life. That incident set the tone of his life. He vowed at thirteen, that he would never treat anyone with disrespect as long as he lived and he would never let another lynching happen in his presence again. He didn't know how he would stop that kind of cruelty but he vowed he would find a way.

Chapter 17

Isaiah Shields works as janitor at the Willow Park School where Josette does her substitute teaching. He's a hard worker and everyone at the school likes him. He keeps the school spotless. Each day when the children come to school, the windows are clean, the floors shine and each desk has been wiped off. When the children and teachers come in the door, a pleasant smell of clean is in the air. A few of the teachers remember the way it was before Isaiah came to work there. The janitor at that time was Mr. Starks. A lazy, snuff dipping slob. He did a poor job of cleaning the school and each time the principal complained to the all white School Board, he was ignored. The teachers and the children cleaned their classrooms but the halls and the bathrooms were filthy. The bathrooms smelled like urine all the time. It was not a good environment for children to learn or teachers to teach.

Everyone thought the principal's complaints fell on deaf ears because the school was for colored children only and the janitor was related to one of the School Board members.

After Mr. Starks died and Isaiah was hired, the school changed for the better. The first day on the job, Isaiah worked all night cleaning the building. The next day when the children and the teachers arrived at school and saw the sparkling windows, the shiny floors and smelled the pleasant aroma of the halls and bathrooms, they were in awe. They couldn't believe it was the same school. Even the gym smelled good. Not much work got done that day but in the days that followed the children looked forward to coming to school. When that first day was over, the children ran home bubbling over with the news of their new clean school. Over the next few days, many of the parents came to school to see what their children were so excited about. Isaiah didn't know it but his work ethic was responsible for the teachers and parents coming together to make a better learning experience for the children.

Soon after Isaiah got the job, he met Esther. She walked to the bus every morning at the same time Isaiah walked to school. The school is only three blocks from where Isaiah lives. The first time he saw her, he was too shy to talk to her. It took him a week just to say hello. That started them talking and in six months they were married at the Willow Park Baptist Church.

At first Esther didn't want to talk to Isaiah. He was too handsome for her. She mistakenly thought he was a ladies man because of his looks. She knew how women ran after handsome men and she wanted no part of that sort of competition. It didn't take her long to realize she was wrong. Isaiah wasn't like that. He didn't know he was handsome. Mentally, he was a little slower than a man his age but he had a pleasant way about him, a beautiful smile and the innocence and trust of a child. Esther loved him from the start and it was she who told him they would be getting married. A year later Solomon was born.

Chapter 18

Esther Shields is sitting on her front porch reading to Solomon just as she does every day. He sits quietly rocking back and forth. He doesn't know the words his mother is reading to him but he listens intently because he loves the sound of his mother's voice. He tries to rock in time to her words like he does to the music he hears at church. Esther and Isaiah never miss Sunday service unless their son is ill.

Solomon is retarded. He has never been to school. His mother and grandmother read to him everyday. This is his only teaching. There is no provision for retarded children of color in the state or local educational system and very little for retarded white children. It will be many years in the future before the educational system will acknowledge these children's needs.

Solomon is nine years old with the mental capacity of a three year old. He can talk a little, walk, dress and feed himself. He just learned to ride a bike. He's bigger than a child of three but smaller than a child of nine. He has large beautiful brown eyes and a crooked smile that show crooked teeth. His eyes keep him from being a homely child.

It's time for Solomon's lunch. Esther goes in the house to prepare something for him to eat. "Momma is gonna make you a sandwich and milk, Solomon. I'll be right back. You stay right here." She's not worried. He usually stays where she leaves him. Today, Solomon didn't stay on the porch. A kitten ran across the yard and Solomon saw it. He left the porch running after it. He was so excited, he made too much noise and frightened the kitten. There is no quiet or graceful way for Solomon to run. Every time he got close, the kitten would run off a little distance until they crossed the road to a grassy field. Solomon is frustrated because he can't catch the kitten so he sits down and cries. After a few minutes the kitten realizes it isn't being chased any more and sits down a little distance away and watches Solomon. They stare at each other for a few minutes. Then the kitten comes to Solomon, climbs in his lap and mews. Solomon is surprised and happy. He gently rubs his hands down the kitten's back. He has a big smile on his face. Then he hears his mother calling him. Solomon stands up and the kitten jumps to the ground. He picks the kitten up and runs to meet his mother. Esther sees him across the road and runs to meet him with tears in her eyes. She and his grandmother had been looking all over for him. They were frantic.

He holds the kitten up for her to see. "Mine Momma, see, see mine!"

Esther is afraid for this tiny animal. Solomon doesn't know his own strength. "Let Momma hold him until we get to the porch. You hold my hand. I'll get him some warm milk."

"No Momma, mine, mine."

"It's all right Solomon. I'll give him back as soon as we get to the porch. I'll hold the kitten. You hold my hand." He hands her the kitten but he never takes his eyes off of it. On the porch Solomon sits down and Esther hands him the kitten. She watches him gently stroke the kitten. She is amazed how gentle he is. Most of the time Solomon is rough and clumsy.

Ruby, Solomon's grandmother, comes around the corner of the house calling Esther. "I can't find him Esther. He's not out back." She's crying and rubbing her hands together. "Oh Esther, where can he be?"

"It's ok Ruby. He's here. He was across the road. Come see what he found."

"Oh thank God! I was real scared. What you got baby? Let Grandma see."

Solomon holds up the kitten. "Mine, mine, Ga ma."

"I see baby." She turns to Esther, "Are you gonna let him keep it? Suppose he hurts it. You know how clumsy he is. It will break his heart if somethin' happened to it."

"Watch him for a few minutes Ruby. See how gentle he is with it. I've never seen him like this before. It's wonderful. Will you get it a saucer of milk.? I'll keep watch. Solomon, Grandma is gonna get the kitty some milk. You eat your lunch."

Esther is delighted. She has never seen Solomon so happy or connected to anything or anyone other than her, his father or his grandmother. She lets him keep the kitten. She wouldn't dare try and take it away. However, she still watches closely when Solomon is playing with it just to make sure he doesn't accidentally hurt it.

Chapter 19

Ruby is Solomon's grandmother and Isaiah's mother. Isaiah was born to Ruby when she was fifteen. She doesn't know who his father is. But, she knows it's one of three boys who grabbed her after school one day, dragged her into the woods and raped her. Ruby was a virgin. She never told anyone. She was too ashamed. When her period didn't come the next month, she knew she was going to have a baby. A baby she didn't want. She hated being pregnant.

At first, she cried a lot because she was afraid to tell her father. She knew her mother would understand. Her mother was the kindest person in town. Everyone in town loved and respected her mother. Ruby and her mother were very close but her mother was timid when it came to her father. He wasn't mean to her but he completely dominated her. She never went against him. When Ruby told him she was pregnant, he became very angry and called her a wayward girl. He's a deacon in the church and was more concerned about being embarrassed than he was about his daughter being raped. He yelled and said she was going to hell. Then he took off his belt to whip her. For the first time in her life Ruby saw her mother stand up to her father.

"Oh no you don't Mr. Shields. Don't you dare lay a hand on this child! I ain't never defied you before but now I say No!"

Ruby's father was more surprised at his wife's rebellion than he was at finding out his daughter was pregnant. He's a superstitious man and he's sure the devil got into his house and corrupted his women folk.

Ruby didn't want the baby she was carrying until he was born and she saw how beautiful he was. His eyes were big, dark brown and beautiful. He had long eyelashes and a rich chocolate brown skin color. He was a handsome child and grew to be a handsome man. It didn't matter to Ruby or her mother that Isaiah was slower than the other children his age. He had a winning smile and a friendly personality. Everyone who met him liked him immediately. Even his grandfather came to love him. It was hard to resist his smile. When he was old enough to go to Sunday School, his grandfather proudly took him every week. His embarrassment was long forgotten.

As a young man Isaiah was a hard worker but because he was slow he only worked at menial jobs. His employers took advantage of him by working him extra hours and not paying him. They bragged about him being a good worker. They even said he was the best they ever had but that didn't stop them from cheating him. Isaiah never complained. He knew what was going on and when he got frustrated and had enough, he just never went back.

He got the job as janitor at Willow Park Elementary School because of his grandfather. Isaiah's grandfather worked for a member of the school board and he asked his employer to hire Isaiah after Mr. Starks died.

Isaiah got the job and kept it until he was an old man.

Chapter 20

One night after Solomon was put to bed, Esther and Isaiah were sitting on the porch talking. Esther says, "Isaiah, have you noticed how gentle Solomon is with his kitten? I've never seen him so connected to anythin' before. He feeds it, pets it and puts it out so it won't go to the bathroom in the house. He even watches until it's finished doin' its business. When it finishes scratchin' in the dirt, he gently picks it up and brings it back in the house. He's learned another thing Isaiah. Every year he learns somethin' new."

Isaiah takes his wife's hand, "Yeah Esther, I see what he does. It's all good but you know he's always gonna need someone to take care of him."

"I know Isaiah, I just want him to be able to do all that he can. We can't ever think he can't do somethin' without givin' him the chance. He's a little older now maybe he can learn to count a little. You always talk about Miss Fuller and what a good teacher she is, maybe she'll come teach Solomon if you ask her. I've saved a little money to pay her. Will you ask her?"

"She don't work every day Esther. I'll ask her when I see her but don't get your hopes up she might not want to do too much work now. She retired a few years back."

"She might though, ask her to come meet Solomon. He has a special way about him. She might say yes."

It's now Friday. Josette has finished another day of substitute teaching and is looking forward to going to the lake with Caleb on Saturday. She's on her way out the door when she hears someone calling her.

"Miss Fuller, Miss Fuller, wait up a minute please." Isaiah is hurrying down the hall to catch up with her. "Miss Fuller, can I ask you somethin'.?"

"Of course Isaiah, walk with me to my truck while we talk. What can I do for you?"

"My wife told me to ask you to come see our little boy Solomon. You've seen him a couple times. I bring him to school with me sometimes. He don't come to school like the other kids. He can't talk but his momma and grandma read to him every day. He likes that. He sits real quiet and listens." Isaiah is nervous and stumbling over his words.

Josette touches his arm to calm him down. "Slow down Isaiah, you're talking too fast. I know your little boy. He's a beautiful child. Is something wrong?"

"Oh no Miss Fuller, he's fine. My wife wants to know if you could teach Solomon to count. Maybe you could spare a few hours a week to teach him. He's limited Miss Fuller but if he could count just a little, I think my wife would feel better. She worries about not doin' enough for him. He's a good boy Miss Fuller. He won't give you no trouble. He only knows his momma, grandma and me. We think he needs to see other people up close. That's why I bring him to school sometimes. So he could see other kids but now he has a cat and he won't leave it."

Josette knows Isaiah's little boy is retarded and she has not had any experience teaching children like him. She's a little hesitant but she says, "I would love to come see Solomon. Is tomorrow morning all right?"

"Yes Ma'am! I'll tell my wife. Thank you Miss Fuller."

"Isaiah, I'm not sure I can help him. I'll let you know after I've seen him. I've never taught a child who couldn't talk before. He may need someone with more experience than I have."

Isaiah is all smiles as he says, "Miss Fuller I see you with the kids here. You're a good teacher. Even if you teach him a little my wife will be happy."

"Ok Isaiah, I'll see you tomorrow." Josette drives off thinking about Caleb. They had planned to go to the lake early tomorrow and spend the day. They will still go but they'll be delayed a little. She's sure Caleb will understand.

Josette loves teaching and considers herself good at what she does. However, teaching a retarded child who can't talk might be too much for her. She's afraid of failing and having to see disappointment on the faces of Isaiah and his wife. This feeling of insecurity about teaching is something new to her. She doesn't like it. She tells herself to stop worrying and decide what to do after she visits with Solomon.

The next morning Josette wakes refreshed. She's ready when Caleb knocks on the door.

The sight of Josette always brings a smile to his face. "Good mornin' Sweetheart. I've been waitin' all week for today. I stopped and filled the thermos with coffee and bought bacon and egg sandwiches for us to eat on the way."

"Good morning Caleb, come in. You always think of everything. I could use some coffee. We have to eat here before we leave. There's something I have to do first."

Caleb looks disappointed. "You haven't changed your mind about goin' to the lake have you?"

"No, no! I'm looking forward to going just as much as you are. I promised Isaiah I would come by this morning and meet his little boy. He wants me to teach him to count. It will only take a little while. Do you mind? You can drop me off and come back and pick me up or you can wait. Then we will have the whole day to ourselves."

Caleb smiles. "I don't mind sweetheart. It doesn't matter if we go a little later."

They drink their coffee and eat their sandwiches at Josette's kitchen table. She tells Caleb about Isaiah's child and his request.

On the way to Isaiah's house, Josette is quietly thinking about Solomon. Josette says, "Caleb, I'm looking forward to the challenge presented to me with this child but I'm also worried. I may not be up to it. I've never taught a retarded child before. If I take the job, I'll have to do some serious research before I give Isaiah my word. I hope I can help them."

Caleb takes her hand and kisses it. "Don't worry so much Josette. You're a fine teacher. That little boy will be blessed to have you."

When they get to Isaiah's house, the family is sitting on the porch. Isaiah comes to meet her. "Thank you for comin' Miss Fuller. This here's my wife, Esther, and this is Solomon."

At the sound of his father saying his name, Solomon looks up and smiles. His smile lights up his face and big beautiful eyes overwhelm his crooked teeth.

Josette sits on the steps next to Solomon and says, "Hi Solomon, I'm Miss Fuller. I'm pleased to meet you. Your Daddy has told me so much about you. He told me you have a kitty."

At hearing the word kitty, Solomon jumps up and runs to his Mother yelling, "Mine Momma, mine, mine!"

"She puts her arm around him saying, "It's all right Solomon, your kitty's takin' a nap. He'll be back."

He startled Josette when he jumped up so suddenly. "Did I do something to upset him Mrs. Shields? I didn't mean to. Is he all right?"

"Oh no, Miss Fuller, don't worry. When he doesn't see his kitten, he thinks someone took it. That's why he yells, "mine". The truth is, the poor little thing just hides for a while to get a rest from Solomon. He'll come back in a bit. Solomon never puts him down. I was afraid at first. We thought he might accidentally hurt it but you should see him. He is so gentle, so gentle. We're amazed."

Josette is relieved. She is also pleased because now she believes she can teach this child how to count. From what Isaiah said, she thought Solomon couldn't talk at all. She tells his parents, "I don't know how far Solomon will learn to count but I believe he can learn some. It may take a while but if we make it a game and you reinforce what I do when I'm not here, he might do well. Isaiah, come see me after school on Monday. I'll have a plan all worked out by then." She walks over to where Solomon is and says, "Good-by Solomon, it was nice meeting you. I'll see you next week." She leaves Isaiah and his family on the porch waving good-by.

She has a good feeling because she has a chance to successfully teach a child that some thought of as un-teachable. This child is special to her and when Caleb arrives to pick her up she has a big smile on he face. On the ride to the lake she tells Caleb of the ideas bouncing around in her head. "Caleb, I can teach this little boy. I know I can! I'm so excited! To give him a chance to learn more than he knows now is worth the challenge. Every child should have the opportunity to learn all they can. That's why I became a teacher. Caleb, I saw too much ignorance accepted by too many. No child should be denied the chance to do his best. Solomon's parents are committed to making sure he can do all that he can. Each step forward he makes delights them. Yet, they know he's limited and accepts him and loves him the way he is. These are very special people Caleb, very special people."

"Wow Josette, I never saw this side of you before. Of course you're gonna teach that little boy to count. Every one says you're the best teacher in Willow Park. That family is lucky to get you."

"Thank you Caleb."

"Josette, I'm curious about somethin'. Why would someone name their retarded child Solomon? Wasn't Solomon the wisest man in the world in the Bible?"

She's surprised at his question and replies sharply "What do you suggest they call him Caleb? These are religious people. Most people with a deep faith name their children from the Bible. Who knows, maybe they didn't realize he was retarded at the time he was born. Every parent believes their baby is the smartest and the most beautiful. They ooh and aahh over every stage of development. Think about their heartbreak when they realize their baby isn't developing the way he should and will never be like other children. Think about how they felt when he didn't sit up when he was suppose to or crawl and walk when he was supposed to. Esther said he didn't walk until he was almost three and didn't learn to ride his bike until recently. Now he's nine and she wants him to be able to count. Each time that little boy accomplishes anything at all his parents are happy. That happiness is no different from parents who have children who develop at a normal pace. They don't expect a lot Caleb. They just want him to be able to do all that he can. I admire these people Caleb, I really do. Esther and Ruby read to Solomon every day. They know in their hearts he will never learn to read but that doesn't stop them. They go on and on. Esther knows Solomon's ability to count is small but if he could just do a little they will be happy. I've never seen a family so committed to a child before. That little boy is blessed and so am I."

"I didn't mean no harm askin' Josette. In my line of work I didn't have much to do with kids. I just wondered. It seemed strange to me. I don't know much about the Bible either so maybe I should keep my mouth shut."

"It's all right Caleb. I didn't mean to speak so sharply to you. I know your heart and I love you for it. Thank you for listening to me go on and on about this child."

Chapter 21

Solomon's lessons have been going on for three months. Josette asked Isaiah to paint some clothespins the primary colors, red, yellow and blue plus the color green. In her lesson plan she decided to combined color with counting. At first she wasn't sure if she was getting through to Solomon. He only smiled when she talked to him. Then, whenever the kitten appeared, the day's lesson was lost. All Solomon wanted to do was play with the kitten. There was no way to keep his attention when the kitten was around. After several of these interruptions, Esther closed the kitten up in Solomon's room until his lesson was over. Josette was beginning to think he would not grasp the concept of color and counting when something exciting happened.

The day's lesson is over. She and Solomon pack the clothespins in the basket they use for class. She takes him by the hand and he carries the basket. They go to the backyard where Esther is hanging the wash on the clothesline. "I'm leaving now Esther. I'll be here again on Saturday morning."

"Thank you Miss fuller. Solomon, do you want to help me hang the wash?" He runs to his Mother and hugs her. "He always helps me by giving me one clothes pin at a time. It takes me twice as long to hang these clothes but he has so much fun, I take the time." She tells Solomon, "Give Momma one baby." And points to the laundry basket where the clothespins are. Solomon runs back to where Josette is and gets a blue clothespin from his basket. He runs back to his Mother waving it in the air. "Boo Momma boo." He repeats this until she takes it from him.

Josette whoops with joy. "Oh praise the Lord! Esther do you know what just happened? He connected! I've been teaching him colors too and I always say this one is blue. When you said give me one, he came back to his basket for the blue clothespin. This is working Esther, this is working!"

Esther bends down and hugs Solomon with tears in her eyes. "You're a good boy. Solomon. Tomorrow we'll go to town and buy you a toy. I knew you could do it. I can't thank you enough Miss

Fuller. I know this is a small victory but it's still a victory for him. I can't wait to tell his father."

"Esther, this is a victory for us all. I'm so happy to help. I'll see you on Saturday." Josette leaves Esther and Solomon with a light heart and a big smile on her face. She can't wait to tell Caleb.

Chapter 22

That was Wednesday. On Thursday, Esther and Isaiah were so excited about Solomon's progress that they played with him and his clothespins all day. Isaiah stayed home from work that morning so he could be with his son. They were doing fine until the kitten appeared. Then Solomon forgot all about his parents. The kitten captured his complete attention. Only when the kitten ran away to get some rest from Solomon were Esther and Isaiah able to get him interested in counting again. It was a wonderful day in the Shields' household.

That evening Esther tells her husband, "Isaiah, I'm gonna take Solomon to town tomorrow and buy him a toy. He's earned somethin' special. We did the right thing askin' Miss Josette to teach Solomon his numbers. I know he's got a long way to go but he did learn some. I'm grateful for that. We've been blessed and I say thank you to God everyday for this child."

Isaiah puts his arm around his wife's shoulder and says, "What do you think he'll like Esther? It's got to be somethin' special."

"I know. I'll try and find a toy to go along with Miss Josette's teachin' so he won't forget."

Isaiah and Esther go to bed that night happy. They make love and sleep with their arms around each other in a blissful hug. Esther refers to this as her hug of happiness. This is something they will do all of their married life. Whether they make love or not they always sleep in a hug of happiness.

The next day after the morning chores are done and breakfast is over, Esther gets Solomon bathed and dressed for their trip into town. Ruby was suppose to go with them but she had a headache and didn't want to ride a bouncing bus.

It's getting close to noon so Esther decides to give Solomon his lunch before they go. There won't be anyplace in town for them to eat anyway and she refuses to sit on the sidewalk and feed her son with people walking by staring at them. These thoughts start to take away her joy of buying a toy for her child. She talks to herself, "Stop the negative thoughts Esther. Nothin' is gonna spoil our day. This is a great day for me and Solomon." As they are waiting for the bus she tells Solomon, "We'll go in the ten cents store and buy you a toy but first we'll look in the window to see what's there. If we can find somethin' from the display we won't have to stay in there long. We'll go in quickly, buy what we want, then leave."

Solomon looks up at his mother and smiles.

They get off the bus close to the store. It's only two blocks away, a short walk. In the window are lots of toys. Some Esther has never seen before. They all seem so wonderful but not what she wants for Solomon. He wouldn't know what to do with most of them and Esther is sure the cost is more than she could afford anyway. It was Solomon who saw the crayons. The box was open with the crayons spread out in the shape of a fan on top of a coloring book. He was so excited he jumped up and down saying, "Boo Mamma boo, pointing to the crayons.

"Is that what you want baby? Come on let's go in and buy it." The sales clerk looks up when they come in and ignores them. Esther is polite, "Excuse me Miss, I would like to buy the coloring book and crayons you have in the window."

The sales clerk looks at Esther for a few seconds before answering her. "It cost one dollar. Do you have a dollar?"

Esther proudly says, "Yes I have."

"Ok I'll get it for you but don't let your pickaninny touch anythin'." Esther hugs Solomon close to her keeping the anger she feels in her gut under control. She says, "My child's name is Solomon."

The clerk just rolls her eyes and goes to get the crayons and book. When she comes back Esther hands her the dollar. She puts it in the cash draw and walks away.

Esther says, "May I have a bag please."

She looks at Esther with contempt, takes a bag from under the counter, slaps it down on the counter and walks away pretending to work among the merchandise.

Esther thanks her, puts the coloring book and crayons in the bag and walks out the door without a backward glance. She doesn't see the clerk standing there with her hands on her hips with a nasty sneer on her face watching, to make sure Esther doesn't steal anything on her way out.

The clerk goes back to work muttering to her self. "How dare that nigger expect to be waited on by a white woman!" She doesn't like the coloreds coming in the store. If she had her way they wouldn't be allowed in but the owner likes the all mighty dollar too much. He doesn't care where it comes from. Not a native southerner, he doesn't care about its traditions especially if it interferes with his money. The sales clerk hates her job.

Esther is sad walking back to the bus stop. She has lived in the south all her life but each encounter she has with bigotry eats at her soul. She swore nothing would spoil her happiness today but she let a hate filled woman get her angry. This is one of those days that makes her glad Solomon doesn't understand the hate directed toward colored people. After a few minutes the anger subsides and she tells her self getting angry at ignorance doesn't do any good. She smiles at Solomon and says, "Here Baby, you carry your present." Solomon takes the bag in one hand and holds onto his mother's hand with the other. He swings his bag and tries to skip down the sidewalk. Esther smiles at her son and makes a game of skipping with him. The unpleasant clerk is forgotten.

The bus stop is on the next corner. Just as Esther and Solomon get there, the Spinner Brothers stumble around the corner and Boots bumps into Esther. She pulls Solomon close to her as she backs away apologizing. "I'm sorry sir. I guess I wasn't lookin' where I was goin'."

Boots doesn't answer her. He stands there staring at Solomon in a drunken fog. "Hecky, look at him. He looks funny."

Hecky, just as drunk as his brother, bends down to look Solomon in the face. Bending down throws off his equilibrium and he almost falls. He grabs on to his brother laughing. "He's a little dummy Boots. Hey Mammy can your pickaninny talk?"

Esther is frightened, "Please Mister, leave us alone. He's just a little boy. We're on our way home. I said I was sorry."

Hecky ignores Esther's plea and says to his brother, "Hey Boots let's give the dummy a swing."

Esther puts Solomon behind her to protect him as the Spinners wrestle him away from her. Esther is screaming No, No! Solomon has gotten frightened and is crying. Esther puts up a ferocious fight. Hecky gets mad and punches her in the stomach and knocks her down. He grabs Solomon who is screaming. "Hey Boots, catch!" He throws Solomon at his brother. "Give him a swing around. Give him a ride."

Esther is screaming, "No, No you'll hurt him please leave him alone." She gets up and tries to stop Boots but Hecky knocks her down again.

Boots is swinging Solomon around in a circle by his arms and laughing but he is too drunk to keep it up without falling. He quickly gets dizzy and falls. Solomon flies out of his hands and hits the sidewalk hard. He screams in pain as his arm is knocked out of socket and broken. Hecky tries to help Boots up but they are laughing so hard and are so drunk that Boots gets halfway up then falls back down pulling Hecky with him.

Lloyd drives around the corner and sees the Spinners on the ground laughing and Esther, sitting on the ground holding Solomon screaming in pain. He stops the car, gets out and asks, "What's goin' on here?"

Hecky still laughing says, "Nothin' Sheriff the little dummy fell. We was just playin' with him. He ain't hurt."

"He's makin' a mighty big fuss for nothin' to be wrong." He bends down to look at Solomon. "Is he all right?"

Esther is still crying and trying to comfort her child. "I don't think so Sheriff. His arm looks funny. He won't let me touch it and he can't lift it."

"Did these two do this?"

"Yes Sheriff, they were swingin' him around. I tried to make them stop but they wouldn't. They knocked me down and took him away from me." Esther starts to cry again.

Lloyd turns to the Spinner Brothers who he dislikes intensely and says, "What's the idea pickin' on a little kid? Get in the back of the car, both of you. Now! You're goin' to jail!"

Hecky yells at Lloyd. "We ain't done nothin' Sheriff. He's just a little dummy. Why you takin' his side?"

"Shut the hell up and get in the back of the car. I ain't gonna tell you again."

"Esther you and your boy get in the front and I'll drop you at Dr. Marshall's office. Then I'm takin' these two to jail."

Hecky and Boots are in the back seat still laughing. "Hey Boots, did you see that booger go flyin'?"

"Yeah Hecky, he was flyin' high."

These two despicable drunks are enjoying themselves in the back seat while a frightened mother hugs and rocks her child in the front.

When they reach Dr. Marshall's office, Lloyd carries Solomon in. The Doctor hears the commotion and comes out to see what's going on. He immediately takes Solomon from Lloyd.

Lloyd tells Esther, "I'm sorry about what that trash did to your boy. I'll see to it that they stay in jail for a time. They won't bother you again be sure of that."

"Thank you Sheriff." Esther was afraid of Lloyd at first because of his reputation. He is said to be mean and hateful toward colored people but now she's grateful for his help. She doesn't know how she would have gotten her child to Dr. Marshall's office without him.

Lloyd drives his car with all the windows rolled down trying to get rid of the stench emanating from the Spinner Brothers. It only takes a few minutes at full speed to reach the station. Lloyd yells at the Spinners, "Get the hell out of this car now!"

Hecky spits at Lloyd and lucky for him, he missed. "I'm comin' Sheriff. ain't no reason for you to be so hostile. We ain't done nothin' wrong."

Lloyd grabs Hecky by the throat and pulls him face to face. "If you ever spit at me again you pig, I'll cut out your tongue and feed it to the dogs! Now get in the station and you better not say another word."

Hecky and Boots are still drunk when they stagger into the station. Lloyd's words scares them so they're quiet until left alone in the cell. They collapse on cots that are fastened to the wall to sleep off the effect of the rotgut whiskey they have been drinking. When they wake up it's dark outside. They have a furry taste in their mouth, a headache, and a foul smell surrounds them. This smell of sour whiskey, unwashed bodies, rotten teeth and urine fill the cell. This smell floats down the hall leading to the front of the jail where Jake is sitting. The urine smell comes from Boots. He wet his pants while passed out.

He calls his brother, "Hecky, I'm wet. Call the Sheriff and ask him for a pair of dry pants for me. Maybe he'll let us go home now. It's dark out. We been here a long time." Boots is sitting on his cot hunched over with his arms between his legs trying to get warm. His urine soaked pants are cold and his whining is getting on Hecky's nerves.

"Yeah Boots, we'll call him but first we gotta make a plan to get even with Caleb Carter and let's include Sheriff Lloyd too. Who does he think he is takin' the side of niggers against white men?"

"I don't care about him Hecky. I'm cold. I wanna go home." Boots starts to cry.

Hecky yells at him, "Stop that cryin'! You sound like a baby. Here take my blanket and wrap it around your waist. In a few minutes you'll be warm. Use yours to do the same."

"I can't Hecky, this one's wet too."

"Damn it Boots, stop that whinin'!" Throw the wet one on the floor. You'll be warm in a few minutes."

"Ok Hecky, don't be mad." He wraps the dry blanket around his waist and sits there rocking back and forth. The cell is quiet while Hecky plots revenge on Caleb Carter and Lloyd Wall.

Chapter 23

Hecky is frustrated. His mind can't get beyond his anger. He can't think of a plan to get revenge on Caleb Carter. "Hey Boots, you feelin' better? I can't think of nothin' to get even with that ex sheriff. What about you? We have to think of somethin' that won't get us caught. I'm tired of goin' to jail."

Boots is agitated, "No Hecky, I don't wanna think about him. I'm scared of him. Let's leave him and that gal alone. Let him keep sneakin' around with her. I don't care. We been tryin' to catch her for a long time and we never did. Let him have her. When he gets tired of her then we can go after her again. Maybe then she'll like us better. If we don't tell nobody maybe she'll be more willin'."

"What you mean, don't tell nobody? Do you think anybody cares what a dinge says. It's her word against ours. I wonder if any white folks know the big bad Sheriff is messin' with a dinge." All of a sudden a light bulb flashes in the dim brain of Hecky Spinner. He gets excited. "That's it Boots, that's it. I know how to get even with Caleb Carter. I bet that mean Sheriff Lloyd don't know his friend is messin' with a dinge. He jumps up and starts to yell for Lloyd. "Hey Sheriff, Sheriff," Jake comes instead.

"What the hell is all this racket for? What do you want?" Jake has his hands on his hips glaring at Hecky.

"We got somethin' important to tell Sheriff Lloyd. We want to see him now."

Jake can't stand the smell any longer. He puts his hand over his nose but it doesn't help. "Well, he ain't here now. I'll tell him when he gets back. Maybe then he'll let you boys go. Oh Lord I hope so!" He leaves them still holding his nose and talking to himself. "Why did Lloyd bring these two drunks here? They always drunk. He coulda left them someplace else to sleep it off." Jake closes the door between the cells and the office hoping to block the odor from coming up front. It helps a little. Just as he sits down, Lloyd walks in carrying two bags of food for the prisoners.

"Hey Jake, take this food back to those boys. I'll let them go soon."

"I would Sheriff but I just came from back there. They were raisin' hell callin' you. They said they had somethin' important to tell you. They wouldn't tell me what it was. Why don't you go see what they want?"

"Ok Jake, are they sober now?"

"Yeah, I think so."

Lloyd gets the keys and unlocks the door to the back. As soon as he steps in the hall leading to the cells the foul smell assaults him. It gets worse as he nears the Spinner brothers. "Ok boys, here's your dinner. Jake says you got somethin' to tell me. What is it?"

Hecky jumps up and grabs the bags of food. Boots doesn't move. He has finally gotten warm. Hecky throws him his bag and they tear into the food. They eat fast enough to choke. It's a disgusting sight as they chew with their mouths open and some of the food falls out on to the floor.

Lloyd stands there watching this disgusting sight. "Ok boys, What do you want? I ain't got all day."

Hecky looks at Lloyd and grins with a mouth full of food. "Yeah sheriff, I was wonderin'. Have you met Caleb's girlfriend yet?"

Lloyd didn't expect this and it took him by surprise. The look of surprise on Lloyds face encourages Hecky to go on. His grin gets wider and more food drops out of his mouth.

"What business is Caleb's lady friend to you? Why are you askin' me about her?"

"Oh, it ain't nothin' to me. Nope, it ain't nothin' to me if he wants to mess around with a dinge. I wouldn't be bothered myself. A dinge is a dinge. I don't care how pretty she is. He might decide to bring her home with him one night. Don't you live with Caleb Carter? He might even let you share her one night. I hear they mighty good in bed. I know she likes white men's hands on her. Why, one time when me and Boots was younger, we both had our hands all over her. She loved it!"

Lloyd stands there staring at Hecky. He can't believe what he is hearing.

Hecky and Boots seeing how these hateful words affect Lloyd, start to laugh. They are laughing so loud and hard, they don't hear Lloyd unlock the cell and step in. Hecky gets hit with Lloyd's nightstick first. Boots screams and scrambles back in the corner of his cot trying to get away from Lloyd. The blanket that was keeping him warm is forgotten. He's screaming his brother's name calling for help. Lloyd grabs his arm and handcuffs him to the bed. Lloyd is the only one quiet in the cell. His attention returns to Hecky, who is holding his head and screaming cuss words at Lloyd."

Lloyd is furious. "You stinkin' piece of trash. I'm gonna fix you so you don't tell that lie to another livin' soul."

Hecky yells, "It's true, it's true! Ask him, ask him! I got no reason to lie ask him!"

These are the last words Hecky gets out of his mouth. Lloyd puts his nightstick back in his belt and hits Hecky in the mouth with his fist. It's a powerful blow and Hecky sees stars dancing before his eyes as he falls back on the cot. For the next few minutes Lloyd pounds Hecky with his fists until he's unconscious. Then he turns to Boots who is screaming in fear. Boots backs up as far as he can go in the corner. His beating isn't as severe because Lloyd has gotten tired. His arms ache and his hand hurts. He thinks he has broken it. He leaves the cell. His anger somewhat abated because of the pain.

He's unaware Jake saw him hit Hecky over and over again. Jake ran back to the front desk and pretended he didn't see or hear anything. Jake is nervous and has a hard time concealing it from Lloyd when he comes into the office holding his hand.

"Jake take those two home and dump them in their front yard like the garbage they are and clean up that cell. Throw out everything in it and burn it in the back.

Jake's nervousness disappears and his pride takes over. He jumps up out of his chair at Lloyd's command and yells, "Me clean that cell? I ain't no maid! Why can't I get one of them colored gals to clean it?"

Lloyd was on his way out the door when Jake opened his mouth. He spins around and glares at Jake. The look on Lloyd's face scares Jake and he sits back in the chair with a thud, stammering, "Ok sheriff, ok. I'll get right on it." He watches Lloyd closely as he walks out of the office down the street holding his hand. "Oh man, somethin' bad is wrong with Lloyd. I better get these bums out of here before he comes back." He gets the keys and runs back to take Hecky and Boots out of their cells. "Ok boys come on. I'm takin' you home." Then he sees Hecky. He's a bloody mess and he's unconscious. His lips are swollen twice their size. His nose is bleeding and leaning to one side like it's broken. Boots is huddled in the corner of his cot still handcuffed and crying. Jake is nervous once again. He leaves the cell area and rushes to get the car. He then drives to the back of the jail so no one will see him when he brings the Spinners out. Jake is scared and mumbling to himself, "Oh Lord these two look bad maybe I should take them to the hospital. No, I better not. Lloyd said take them home. I'll let their folks take care of them. Oh Lord, this is bad!" Jake releases Boots from the handcuffs but Boots doesn't move. He stays in the corner curled up in the fetal position cowering in fear. Jake yells at him, "Come on Boots move! Help me with your brother. I'm takin' you home."

"Don't hit me no more sheriff. Please don't hit me no more." Boots is sobbing and pleading with both arms over his head to ward off blows he thinks are coming.

Jake is losing his temper. "Get up Boots! I ain't the Sheriff and I ain't gonna hit you! Now come on help me with your brother."

Slowly Boots lowers his arms and recognizes Jake. "Ok Jake, has the sheriff gone?" He has the look of a trapped animal as he frantically looks around.

"Yeah, yeah he's gone, now come on before he gets back!" Hecky is still unconscious. It's a good thing Lloyd used his fists instead of his nightstick. If he had, Hecky would be dead. It's a struggle to get him out of the cell and into the car and they almost drop him. Boots has to get in the car first and pull Hecky in while Jake holds his feet. They manage to get him on the back seat. Boots has to sit on the floor. Jake takes off with sirens screaming all the way to the Spinner home. Old man Spinner hears the sirens coming close so he comes out to the porch to see where it's going. He's surprised to see the police car speed into his driveway and slam on the brakes.

Jake jumps out calling, "Mr. Spinner come with me. We have to get your boys to the hospital quick!" On his way to dump the Spinners in their front yard, Jake changed his mind. He didn't like the way Hecky was breathing. He sounded like air in a wind tunnel. Jake was afraid Hecky would die while in his custody. The hospital was in the next town but it took him less than five minutes to get there.

Jake's decision saved Hecky's life. He had several fractured ribs from the severe beating he took from Lloyd and one of them punctured his lung. The emergency room clerk tried to get information from Jake about what happened. All Jake would say was, "I found them on the street all beat up. The sheriff will be here later with the details. I have to go." Jake ran out and left the clerk and a nurse standing there confused.

The nurse asks, "What's the matter with him? Did you get any information from him?"

"No I didn't but I think that older man over there is with the patients. He came in with the Deputy."

"Thank you, I'll take care of this now." She leaves the clerk to go speak to Mr. Spinner.

Chapter 24

Lloyd leaves the station exhausted from beating Hecky. Blood is on his clothes and thoughts about what Hecky told him are racing through his mind. It can't be true! Josette can't be colored. Caleb wouldn't sleep with a colored woman. He knows many white men, married and unmarried, have colored girlfriends but not Caleb. He's morally superior to these men. He never talks trash about anyone and he has never shown any interest in any woman in town. Why then was Josette sitting at the kitchen table having dinner with Caleb? That was a surprise. If what Hecky said is true that she likes both colored and white men then Caleb should know this. No, no this can't be true! Lloyd finds himself getting upset again. He tries to calm down and wait until he talks to Caleb. He's always been able to talk to him about anything. This time won't be any different. He'll be home soon. First, he has to change clothes and wash off Hecky's blood. Lloyd can't bear the thought of putting those clothes on again so he puts them in a garbage bag and throws them away.

When Caleb comes home, Lloyd is stretched out on his bed with one hand under his head. He's been like that for a while unable to sleep because his other hand hurts too much.

When Caleb comes home, he stops at Lloyd's door. "Hey Lloyd, just came to say good night."

"Wait Caleb, I need to talk to you. Let's talk in the livin' room."

"Sure Lloyd, what's the matter? You look upset." Caleb begins to be concerned. He has not seen Lloyd this nervous since he was a kid.

When they get to the living room, Lloyd paces the floor for a few minutes before speaking. "Caleb I heard somethin' today I can't believe."

"What are you talkin' about Lloyd? What did you hear?"

"I'm talkin' about Josette. I was told today that she ain't white. You been datin' a colored woman Caleb. She tricked you. She ain't white. She's been messin' with colored men and white men. I'm sorry Caleb I don't mean to hurt you. I thought you should know."

"Slow down Lloyd, you're gettin' upset about nothin'. Josette didn't trick me. I didn't know she was colored at first but she told me shortly after we met. It makes no difference to me what she is Lloyd. I'm in love with Josette. For the first time in my life I find myself in love. I don't know who told you lies about her but don't believe them Lloyd. They ain't true. She's the finest woman I've ever met. She's honest and beautiful and I love her. I've asked her to marry me."

Lloyd is stunned, "Marry you! You gonna marry her? Suppose what they say is true."

"Calm down Lloyd. Who told you all this? I guess I shoulda told you myself, then this wouldn't be such a shock to you. I'm askin' again Lloyd who told you this?"

Lloyd sits down with a thud. The shock of what he just heard weakened his knees. He softly says, "The Spinner brothers. They said they had been with her."

"That explains it, Lloyd. Don't believe what that trash says. They lied to get back at me. I stopped them from botherin' Josette a couple months ago. The only thing they said that's true is, she's colored. I know that and I don't care. I love her and I'm gonna marry her."

They sit there for a few minutes in silence. Lloyd gets up and says, "I'm goin' to bed. I'll see you tomorrow. I'm tired." He has to get out of Caleb's presence. His anger is slowly heating up his body. He doesn't want Caleb to see how he feels. As he leaves the room with his back to Caleb he says, "This is the south Caleb. Where can you live in peace with a colored wife?" He doesn't wait for an answer.

Other people have noticed Lloyd changing but they thought it was because of the stress of his job. It's not easy being a sheriff. Tonight is the first time Caleb noticed the strange look in his eyes and his nervous way of moving. This starts Caleb worrying. He wonders if Ellie May's betrayal has caused more damage than he previously thought. He goes to bed and sleeps badly. He can't get Lloyd off his mind.

Chapter 25

Josette leaves Isaiah's house running with Solomon's screams ringing in her ears. She gets in her truck and a few blocks down the road she pulls off to the side and cries. All the years she has been teaching have been good years. Never in all those years has a child screamed in fright at the sight of her. She was making progress with Solomon and had grown to love that little boy. Sometimes she thought he didn't understand what she said. Then, just as she was trying to find another way to make him understand, he would surprise her. He never got it all but she was delighted with what he did get. Repetition and patience reached him but in his time not hers. She tried to figure out what his timetable was but she could not. Sometimes his brain processed information in hours and sometimes in days. She was always surprised.

Finally her tears stopped and anger took over. Caleb told her of Solomon's abuse by the Spinners. When she saw him with his little arm strapped to his body, she was shocked. He looked so fragile. How could someone do this to a child? Then he started screaming when she approached him. She became frightened for him. She was afraid he would re-injure his arm. His movements were violent as he desperately tries to get away from her. His father picked him up to calm him down. When he couldn't, he took him in the house to his mother. He returned to the porch apologizing to Josette. "I'm sorry Miss Josette. Ever since those boys hurt him, he's afraid of white people. He won't leave the house anymore. I think it's gonna take some time for him to forget."

"I understand Isaiah, I'm so sorry this happened to him. when you think he's over his fear let me know. We can start again whenever you say. Keep helping him with the colors and counting the pins. Don't let him forget the progress he's made."

"He does real good Miss Josette. We make a game of counting those pins. My wife is pleased with what you taught him. We won't forget."

Josette starts to go then turns around and says, "Isaiah, you do know I'm not white don't you?"

"Yes Ma'am. I know, but Solomon don't."

That night, Caleb was disturbed by the look on Josette's face when he came to see her. He could tell she had been crying. Her eyelids were swollen and red. The sad look on her face tore at his heart. "Josette sweetheart, what's the matter? Why have you been cryin'?" Caleb put his arms around her to comfort her. This started the tears flowing again as she clung to him.

"Come Josette, sit with me." He leads her to the couch and holds her on his lap until her tears subside. After a while Caleb asks, Now, are you ready to tell me why you're so upset?"

"He's afraid of me Caleb. That precious little boy is afraid of me. I grew to love him so much. He loves and trusts everyone and now because of those Spinners he knows fear. Because I look white he's afraid of me too. You should have seen the fear in his eyes when I came close to him. His father had to take him in the house to calm him down. I won't be able to teach him any more."

"Josette, give him more time. Maybe it's too soon after his injury. Maybe he'll forget after a while and you can go back to teachin' him. You've done a good job with him. He's just a little kid. He'll forget in time."

Josette didn't answer Caleb. She sat on his lap for a long time without talking. Then she says, "Thank you for being here Caleb. I didn't know what to do. I couldn't stop crying."

Chapter 26

In the next few weeks Josette's spirit heals. Her tears no longer flow when she's alone and thinking about Solomon but she misses his crooked smile, his beautiful eyes and his awkward way of running. Whenever she has a day of substitute teaching, she goes to see Isaiah to ask how Solomon is doing. His words about his son are always encouraging and comforting. He and his wife still diligently teach Solomon his colors and numbers with the clothespins. However, they shield him from seeing any white people. They don't want to see him terrified again. Esther no longer takes him into town. She and Ruby watch him like a hawk and let him go no further than their front yard.

This saddens Josette because she knows Solomon's already small world is shrinking even more instead of expanding like it should.

She tells Isaiah this and he says, "Maybe so Miss Josette, but we want to give him some more time. Don't worry about him, he'll be fine."

Josette still has hopes of teaching Solomon again but for now she accepts his parents decision. They want her to stay away for a little while longer.

Today is Friday and the school week is over. Tonight, Caleb is coming over for dinner. Sitting across the dinner table talking to each other is a pleasure they share. They never seem to run out of things to talk about. This is especially enjoyable for Caleb because he never stayed in a woman's company long enough to talk about anything. He wasn't interested in getting that close. Josette has known this closeness before. She and her late husband used to linger at the dinner table just to talk. This was one of the simple pleasures she missed after he died.

This night, they're still at the dinner table lingering over a cup of coffee, when Caleb says, "Josette, lets go to the lake early tomorrow. There's somethin' I want to show you." Caleb holds up his hand to stop Josette from asking any questions. "Now don't ask me a lot of questions. It's somethin' you haven't seen before. We might change our fishin' spot."

Josette speaks up immediately, "Change our spot? Oh no Caleb, we know every inch of that lake and our spot is the prettiest. We've had wonderful happy times there. Why would we change?"

"Don't get upset sweetheart. I just meant maybe we'll have to change our spot one-day when we come to the lake and someone else is there. We don't own any of that land. We can't run them off no matter how we feel. Tomorrow I'll show you somethin' I know you'll love. I found it by accident and describin' it won't do it justice. You have to see it."

"Ok Caleb, I'll wait but I'm not changing our spot."

They laugh and the subject is dropped until the next morning when they're on the way to the lake. Josette starts the questioning. "Ok Caleb, what did you want to show me? This mystery has been on my mind all night."

Caleb laughs at her. "Don't be so impatient. Wait a little while longer Sweetheart. Did you know there's another road leading to the lake? It's just below where we usually fish but it goes in the opposite direction. I found it one day when I was waitin' for you. I was walkin' around the lake when I saw this dirt road. I followed it to see where it went. You'll see it in a few minutes. It's a one lane road and it ends in a circle. I found out later it's a private road. Look, there it is." Caleb turns off the main road on to what looks like a narrow pathway.

Josette sits up to look out the front window. "Caleb this isn't a road. It's two ruts in the grass. Will we get stuck?"

"No the ground is hard. We won't get stuck. No one except me has been here in a long time. Wait until you see what's at the end."

The road curves and ends in a wide circle in front of a white clapboard cottage with country blue shutters on the windows. A sitting porch extends across the entire front of the house. Brilliant blue morning glories are growing up the porch rails. The yard is overgrown with grass and weeds but a mass of yellow marigolds are blooming among this overgrowth. The house is clearly in need of a paint job but it's still a beautiful sight.

Josette gasps, "Oh my goodness, it looks like a doll house! It's beautiful!

Who does it belong to?"

Caleb smiles at her reaction. "Wait until you see inside." He takes her hand and they walk in. There is no lock on the door. The first thing they see is a large stone fireplace with two red couches on either side facing each other. A long narrow coffee table sits between the couches. The floors are wide hardwood planks stained a rich dark brown. The mantle over the fireplace matches the floor.

This room is large with an arch at each end that leads to another room. The one at the right leads to a combination kitchen and breakfast nook. In front of an eight foot bow window is a maple table and four chairs facing a magnificent view of the lake.

Josette is excited. "Caleb, this is beautiful. How did we come on the lake? I thought we were going in the opposite direction."

"We're on the opposite side of it. This part of the lake is private property. That's why the road is a dirt road. Didn't you notice how it curved around? Come on let me show you the rest."

To the left of the living room is another large room with another fireplace at the end close to the back of the house. A large four-poster bed and an antique dresser are the only pieces of furniture in this room. Although the furniture is old and large, the pieces seem lost because the room is so big. Just before you get to the fireplace there are double French doors that lead out to a flagstone patio. The lake can be seen from here too. Caleb is enjoying himself. The look on Josette's face as he shows her each room is a delight to him. The last room for her to see is the bathroom. It extends almost the entire back of the house and can be entered from the bedroom or the breakfast room. The room is huge. There are two of everything, bathtubs, sinks and toilets all in a light blue color. Separating these two units is a dressing area with mirrors from ceiling to floor on the back wall. At least twenty empty plant stands are all over this room. The walls are white with hand painted blue birds flying all over the room. The reflection of the birds in the mirrors, make it seem like there are hundreds of birds everywhere.

The sun shines in two sets of three windows high up on the wall on each side of the dressing room. Josette is amazed.

"Caleb, this is a wonderful place. I've never seen anything so beautiful. I don't understand this bathroom though. Why two of everything in one room?"

"I wondered about that too, until I found this." Caleb takes a handle that appears to be sticking out of the mirrored wall and pulls. An opaque glass wall slides out and divides the two rooms in half. When it reaches the other side it slips into a six inch slot and no one can tell the wall is not a permanent fixture. The opaque wall has etchings of flying birds across the top.

"Caleb, who owns this marvelous place? Are we trespassing? It doesn't look as if any one has lived here in a very long time. Who keeps the inside so clean? I didn't know places like this were anywhere around here."

"I'm glad you like it Josette. When I first saw it I was just as excited as you are. The people who owned it died a year ago. It's been empty that long. Their children don't want it. They're city people so they put it up for sale. It's been on the market that long and no one has ever been to see it."

"How sad Caleb. I bet their parents loved this place. What will become of it if no one buys it?"

"Some one did buy it. It's no longer on the market."

Then, Josette understands and grabs Caleb's arm, "You bought it! That's why were here! You bought this wonderful place?"

"I did. I bought it for you. I knew you would like it. It needs some work on the outside. A little paint and some yard work will make it like new. I cleaned up the inside but the rest is up to you. Whatever you want in it, go shoppin' and get it. If you want me to go with you I will but I'm not good at that sort of thing.

All I can do is pay for anythin' you want. There's no heat in the house for winter but I guess the two fireplaces heat it up just fine. I'll make sure there's plenty of wood to keep the house warm. I think this house was only used in the summer. We can use it anytime we want."

"Thank you Caleb. I love it. This is wonderful! We'll have fun making it our own. When can we start?"

"As soon as you want. Whenever you want to go shoppin', we'll go."

Then Josette gets quiet. Caleb sees the look on her face. "What's the matter Josette? Is somethin' wrong?"

"I guess not Caleb. When we're together I'm so happy, I tend to forget where we live. What about our neighbors? What happens when they find out a colored woman is their neighbor and living just as good as they are? You know how things are."

"Don't worry Josette. We know almost everyone up here. We haven't had any trouble. I don't think it's gonna be a problem."

"With all your experience as sheriff, you're still in the dark about many things. It's one thing to be nice to colored people and not mistreat them as long as they don't live next door. Something happens even to good people when their life style is upset. Colored people are supposed to stay in their place and I don't think this beautiful house on the lake is one of those places. How many of the people we've met up here know I'm not white?"

Caleb puts his arms around Josette. "Stop worryin' sweetheart. This house is on two acres of land. We don't have any close neighbors. If anythin' happens you will have to trust me to take care of it.

Chapter 27

Josette doesn't take the boys fishing again for two weeks. She has been substituting for an ill teacher. She and Caleb only had one chance to go to the house at the lake. She has had no time to shop for what she would like to put in it. Caleb has been working in the yard clearing the over growth and cleaning out the flowerbeds. They decided on the color to paint the house. It was an easy decision. They wanted to keep it as close to the original as possible. As soon as time allows they will shop for the paint together.

Josette is tired and she misses going to the lake. On her way home Friday, she stops at Cathy's house. When the boys see her, they yell in unison, "Hi Grandma."

"Hello boys. I haven't seen you in a while. I've been working. How would you like to go to the lake tomorrow?"

Stevie and Timmy jump up and down yelling, "Yeah, yeah! What time Grandma?"

Stevie asks, "What time Grandma? Can we go early in the morning? I like the mornings best."

"Sure Stevie, how about seven. Will you be up that early? It's ok with me but we have to ask your mother first."

Stevie's mood instantly changes. "Do we have to ask her Grandma? She's so grouchy lately. You're her mother. You're the boss. Do we have to ask her?"

Josette can't help laughing as she puts her arms around Stevie. "I'm sorry Stevie, I didn't mean to laugh but it doesn't work that way. I'm not your mother's boss. She's all grown up now. I can't tell her what to do. I wouldn't even try. She won't say no. She wants you to be happy and we still have to be polite and ask permission. Do you understand?"

Stevie says, "Yes Grandma," but he still has his doubts.

Josette is angry with Cathy but hides it from her grandsons. If she says no to the boys going fishing with her, she won't make a scene in front of them but Cathy will certainly know how she feels later.

Just then Cathy comes out the front door and instantly recognizes the look of anger on her mother's face. Timmy distracts her with his usual bubbling personality. He's completely unaware of the tension around him.

"Mommy, Mommy, Grandma said we could go fishing with her tomorrow. Can we please, can we?"

Before she answers Timmy, Cathy sees the look in her Mother's eyes that have told her all her life, "Don't you dare girl!" She stumbles over her words and says, "It's ok Timmy you and Stevie can go."

Josette softens up her attitude. "Thank you Cathy. I'll pick the boys up at seven. Don't fix breakfast. We're going to The Griddle and Grits. We plan to be gone all day so don't fix dinner either. Boys, I'll see you in the morning. Ok?"

Not much gets by Stevie. He caught his grandmother's look and his mother's reaction to it. He knew all the time Grandma was the boss no matter what she said. He has a silly grin on his face that he hides from his mother.

Josette plans to take the boys to the house on the lake as soon as Caleb joins them. She hasn't told anyone about it. She wants to surprise the boys first.

The next morning at The Griddle and Grits, the boys are excited and talkative. They're teasing each other about who is going to catch the biggest fish.

Stevie says, "My fish is going to be bigger than yours, Grandma's or Mr. Carter's."

Timmy is surprised. "Is Mr. Carter coming too, Grandma?

"Yes Timmy, Mr. Carter will be there too. Stevie, how did you know Caleb was coming with us? Did I tell you?"

"No Grandma, He's always around when you're at the lake. I think he likes you."

Josette smiles to herself. At least her grandsons approve of Caleb. She pays for their breakfast and says, "Ok boys let's go fishing." They leave the restaurant happy and anticipating a wonderful day fishing and playing. When they get to the lake they unpack the truck and head for their favorite spot. Timmy and Stevie run ahead. Anxious to put down what they're carrying and skip some stones across the water.

Caleb is waiting for them. "Hi Boys, all ready to fish?"

"Yeah Mr. Carter, but first we got a bet. Who can make the most skips over the water with their stones." Timmy shows Caleb his collection of flat stones. "See this stone. It's the best. See how flat it is. The flat ones skip the best."

Josette, her face flushed and smiling says, "Hi Caleb, those rascals ran off and left me. What a beautiful day. Finally, I can relax after a hectic week. I've missed being here with you."

"I missed you too Josette. You don't know how hard it is not to show up at your door every night." He takes her hand and squeezes it. He wants to touch more of her but not in front of her grandchildren.

"It's all right Caleb you can hug me. Stevie told me you like me."

Caleb puts his arms around Josette and says, "That Stevie is a smart young man. I more than like his grandmother. It doesn't look like they're ready to fish yet. Let's sit a while until they finish skippin' stones."

The day is perfect. The sun is shining on the water and everyone is content. Caleb and Josette sit on the shore watching the boys. It's so peaceful. Josette can't believe how happy she is. It's been years since she felt this way. She tells Caleb, "I wish this day could go on forever."

The boys never set their poles to fish. They're having too much fun throwing stones, racing, wrestling on the sand and wading in the water.

At noon Caleb tells Josette he has to leave for a couple hours. "Sweetheart, I have to help Lloyd transfer a prisoner to the county jail in Savannah. I'll be back here around three. Then I'll cook all the fish you and the boys catch and I'll bring back desert. Do you want anythin' else? He sees the look of disappointment on Josette's face.

"I promised him he could call on me any time Sweetheart and this is the first time he's asked. I know it's interruptin' our day. I'll make it up to you, I promise. Will you wait? I'll be back around three. Then we can show the boys the house and cook dinner there. Have you told them yet?"

"No I haven't. I wanted it to be a surprise from both of us. Of Course I'll wait. We had planned to be here all day anyway. A couple hours won't make a difference. Cathy isn't expecting us until late. If the boys ever settle down to fish we may have something for you to cook." She smiles at Caleb to assure him it's all right for him to leave.

Timmy comes running. "Grandma, I'm hungry. Can we have lunch now?"

He stops talking when he sees Caleb getting ready to leave. "Is Mr. Carter leaving Grandma?"

"Just for a little while Timmy. He's coming back."

"I'll only be gone for a little while boys and when I get back I expect to see a lot of fish to cook."

Nothing keeps Timmy down for long. His happy personality shines through as he says, "We're starting right after lunch. We'll catch a whole bunch of fish and mine will be the biggest."

Stevie has been quiet but now his little brother has challenged him. "Oh no you won't! I bet I catch the biggest fish. I'm better at fishing than you are."

Timmy sticks out his chest and points to himself, "No you're not! I'm better than you. Nobody can beat me fishing."

Caleb can't help laughing. "Ok boys I'll tell you what, I'll judge whose fish is the biggest when I get back. Ok?"

Both boys are excited now. They run around chasing each other laughing and then giggling when they see Caleb kiss their grandmother goodbye.

Josette unpacks their lunch and they sit by the shore on a blanket she brought with her. They laugh and talk while they eat fried chicken and biscuits and fried apples. Josette is thinking how happy she is. She feels blessed to have met Caleb and to have two wonderful grandsons. She's at peace in a place she loves. All these good things in her life now still can't keep out the one negative that always seems to creep in when she is most content. She worries about Cathy's attitude toward Caleb and she worries how this is affecting Cathy's mental well being. She knows if she keeps this unhealthy attitude about white men, someday it's going to cause her and her family great harm. Josette doesn't know what to do about it. These thoughts are beginning to spoil her contentment. She shakes her head to get rid of them. She is determined nothing is going to interfere with having a good time today. "Ok boys, are you ready to fish now? All you did this morning was play. Now it's time to fool these clever fish. Who's the smartest, you or the fish?"

The boys jump up. "We are Grandma. We're smarter than any old fish." They get their poles and dig around in the bait box for the biggest worm. After Stevie sets his pole, he says, "Do you want me to set your pole Grandma? I'll bait the hook for you."

"No thank you Stevie. I'll just sit here and watch for a while."

They settle down and for the first time today the boys are quiet as they wait for a fish to bite. It's so peaceful. Josette dozes off.

She wakes up alarmed. Stevie is shaking her. "Grandma, Grandma wake up, I smell them Grandma, wake up!"

"My goodness Stevie, I'm awake. What's the matter?"

Stevie is nervous and frantically looking around. "I smell them! The Spinners, I smell them! They stink something awful. You can smell them before you can see them. Let's go Grandma, Let's go!"

Josette jumps to her feet and looks around. She can't smell them like Stevie but usually they can be heard before they can be seen because they're so loud and vulgar.

"Ok Stevie let's pack up."

"No Grandma they're too close! Leave everything we'll come back later. Come on Timmy we have to go."

Timmy, seeing the look on his brother's face, gets scared, drops his pole and runs to his grandmother's side. Josette is still looking around. She can't see or hear anything that would alert her to the Spinners presence. "Are you sure Stevie? I don't hear anything."

Stevie grabs his grandmother's arm. "Hurry Grandma, I'm sure!"

They leave everything on the ground and run for the truck. Stevie is frantic and Timmy is crying. Just before they reach the road where the truck is parked, Hecky Spinner jumps out in front of them. Josette is terrified. She let her happiness dull her senses and she became less aware of her surroundings. All her life, when away from home, she kept her senses honed to a fine edge. She was always alert to possible danger to her or to her children.

Hecky stands in front of her grinning. "Where you goin' pretty Josette? You ain't leavin' so soon, are you? We just got here. Me and Boots was comin' to your party."

Stevie yells at Hecky, "You leave my grandma alone!"

Josette hugs the boys to her. "What do you want? Get out of my way!"

Hecky still grinning and showing rotting teeth says, "We want you Josette. We been waitin' a long time. We gonna show you how good a white man is. You gonna like it, pretty Josette." He reaches out to grab her and Stevie hits him in the nose with a rock. Timmy throws his rock too but he misses.

Josette grabs each boy by an arm and tries to run around Hecky as he examines his bleeding nose but Boots is too fast for her. He grabs both boys by the collar and they all fall backwards on the ground. Boots jumps on the boys and beats them with his fists until they're unconscious. Hecky forgets his bleeding nose and hits Josette so hard, he knocks her out. He picks her up and calls his brother. "Come on Boots. We got her now. Leave them, we don't want them." He carries Josette until he gets tired, to a place deep in the woods that surround the lake. He dumps her on the ground and they stand there looking at Josette. They can't believe they have captured her after all the years of chasing her.

Boots is very excited. "What we gonna do with her now Hecky? She sure is pretty." Then he gets alarmed as Josette moans. "She's comin' to Hecky. Don't let her run away."

Hecky bends over to look in Josette's face. "She ain't gettin' away this time Boots. She ain't comin' to. She's still out. Let's see if she's the same color all over. Help me take off her clothes." They get down on their hands and knees and strip Josette's clothing off, throwing them away a piece at a time. They sit there looking at her naked body. Then Hecky says, "Boots, we been tryin' to catch this dinge for a long time but man oh man look at her. Its been worth the wait. She's the prettiest gal I ever seen and look, she's the same color all over. Ain't no black on her nowhere."

Boots is rubbing his hands together and licking his lips when he asks, "Can I touch her Hecky?"

"Sure Boots go ahead. Feel her tits. Ain't they pretty?"

Boots reaches over and tentatively touches Josette's breasts. He jumps at the first touch. It felt so good. He tries it again. This time he gets brave and grabs both breasts in his hands, rubbing and kneading. "Oh Hecky, she feels good. her tits are nice and smooth. Them whores don't let me touch them here. This is better than the whores Hecky. Can I do more?"

"Not yet Boots. It's my turn now. He leans over and kisses Josette on the mouth and at the same time squeezes her nipples. His foul breath and the pain in her breasts wakes her. She comes to screaming and kicking. Hecky puts his hand over her mouth to quiet her.

"Shut up or I'll knock you out again!" Boots is holding her down by both ankles while Hecky straddles her. "Shut up all that noise. We ain't done nothin' yet. Don't worry about them pickaninnies. They're fine. Now you co-operate with us or we'll find them some other time and kill them. You understand?" A big grin appears on Hecky's face. "You gonna like what we do." He takes her hand and puts it on the front of his pants. "Feel that? It's nice and hard just for you. I promise it'll be better than any nigger you ever had. You the prettiest dinge I ever seen. How come you ain't got no black on you?"

Josette's next words stun Hecky. "I'm not colored, never have been."

Hecky jumps up so quick he almost falls over. "What the hell you sayin'? You ain't colored?"

"No! I fell in love with a colored man and I had to say I was colored so we could get married. No body questioned me." No one questioned Josette because half white babies are born every year to colored women. Some of these women are victims of rape. Others have to sell their bodies to white men to feed the children they already have. Then there are the ones that truly believe their white lovers, love them. And, that may be true but the South won't let them live in peace. So these relationships are doomed and eventually fall apart.

Hecky is furious. He hits Josette in the face several times calling her a nigger lovin' whore.

Boots is taken by surprise. "What you doin' Hecky? Why you hittin' her like that? I thought we was gonna get some. You didn't say nothin' about beatin' her up."

Hecky's anger turns on his brother. "Shut the hell up Boots! She ain't colored! She's a white whore. She been humpin' colored men. She's spoiled! I ain't gonna hump no spoiled white woman. I ain't goin' behind no nigger. She ain't good enough for us. Gimme your belt, we'll tie her up and leave her here."

Boots is disappointed. He wanted to touch her again and relieve the hardness in his pants. "Can't I just get a little bit Hecky? She felt so good."

"Hell no! I told you she's spoiled. Take off your belt and tie her ankles."

Boots does as his brother tells him but Hecky didn't see Boots reach up and put his hand between Josette's legs. That little feel did Boots a world of good. It released the tension in his pants and when he and Hecky left the scene, he was sticky and wet.

Hecky had no release until later just before they left the woods. His hardness started to hurt and he had to relieve himself. He's furious at Josette. He's been chasing her all these years for nothing.

Chapter 28

Caleb returns to the lake a little after three. He stopped at the diner and bought desert. He purchased some of every kind they had. He's whistling a happy tune and smiles when he sees Josette's truck still in the same spot. He didn't want to leave but he had promised Lloyd he would help him out and the trip to Savannah went smoothly. Happy to be back at the lake, he hurries up the path. He almost missed Stevie. As he passed him, out of the corner of his eye he saw a small shoe just off the path. He turned around to pick it up, wondering where it came from. Then he saw Stevie. His face is swollen and a mass of bruises. "Oh my God! Stevie, wake up! Who did this? Where's Josette and Timmy?"

Stevie opens his eyes and starts to cry. "Find Timmy Mr. Carter. He's around here somewhere."

"Ok Stevie, I'll find him. Then I'll take you both to Dr. Marshall's. Do you know where your grandmother is?"

"They took her Mr. Carter. We couldn't get away." Stevie starts to cry again.

"Calm down Stevie. I'm here now. I'll find them." He lifts Stevie and carries him to his car and puts him on the back seat. "I'll be right back. Don't you move. I'm goin' back for Timmy." Caleb runs back to where he found Stevie and hears Timmy crying. He's a little further off the path. If he had not found Stevie first, he could have missed him. This is a frightening thought. He carefully examines Timmy before lifting him. His arm is at an odd angle. Caleb assumes it's broken, so he is very careful when he picks Timmy up. Though Caleb was very gentle, Timmy still screamed in pain.

He rushes the boys to Dr. Marshall's office. When he gets there he takes Stevie in first. "Dr. Marshall, there's another boy in my car. Somebody beat them bad. I think the other boy has a broken arm. Maybe you better see him before he's moved again. I don't want to hurt him any more."

Dr. Marshall, grabs his bag and rushes out to Caleb's car. Before he moves Timmy, he examines him carefully then gives him a shot to relieve his pain.

Timmy is only half conscious. Dr. Marshall takes his time to make sure no more damage is done to Timmy's arm while he brings him inside. "I know these boys Caleb. Who did this?"

"I don't know Doctor but they were with their grandmother and she's still missing. I'm goin' back to find her. Will you get in touch with the boy's parents?"

"Sure Caleb, you go on. I'll take care of the boys first then I'll call. When you find their grandmother bring her to me so I can check her out too."

Caleb leaves Dr. Marshall's office running. He breaks the speed limit getting back to the lake. He stumbles around in the area where he found the boys calling Josette. When he gets no answer, his heart beats rapidly with fear. He runs to the lake shore where he left her and the boys fishing. They left everything. The poles are on the ground with the lines still in the water. The blanket is messed up and the picnic basket is open and on its side. Some food is still in the basket. It appears they left in a hurry or someone surprised them and they couldn't get away. The only ones Caleb knew Josette to run from are the Spinner brothers. Caleb begins to shake with anger. He tells himself to calm down and think like a lawman. Use your years of training and think logically. That's the only way to find Josette. Finding her is more important than his anger, or fear, or revenge. He'll take care of them later. Caleb stands there looking around. He isn't sure which way to go. He goes back to where he found the boys. Now that he has calmed down a bit, he becomes the sheriff he used to be. He can see broken limbs and trampled grass leading away from the lake. He follows these clues quietly at first. Then he realizes who ever did this wouldn't wait around so he starts to call Josette. He calls, then listens, calls, then listens for about an hour. He's getting desperate. He has to find her. He knows she's here somewhere. He can't see the lake anymore. Did he pass her? Is she dead? Is that why she's not answering? Oh dear God no! All of these things are running through his mind and it's a struggle to keep from having a panic attack. He starts to yell Josette's name again. This time the desperation can be heard in his voice. He stops and listens for a few minutes. Then he hears her.

"Caleb, help me! Caleb, I'm here!"

"Josette, keep callin' sweetheart, I'm comin'. I'll find you. He listens closely to where her voice is coming from and finds her. Her voice had gotten weak. A few more minutes and she would have passed out again. He is shocked at what he sees. Josette is naked on the ground with her arms fastened behind her back with a belt and her ankles are strapped together with another belt. Her face is a mass of bruises and her lips are swollen twice their size. He immediately falls at her side and frees her ankles. "Josette I'm gonna turn you a little to free your arms. Are you in pain?"

"I'm ok Caleb. I don't think anything is broken."

"I'll be as gentle as I can, then I'm takin' you to Dr. Marshall's."

Josette has fear in her voice, "No Caleb, we have to find the boys. I'm afraid they hurt them."

"Hush Sweetheart, I found the boys. They're at Dr. Marshall's. He's takin' good care of them."

"My clothes Caleb, I can't go like this."

"Don't worry about your clothes. I've got a blanket in the car. We can't waste time lookin' for them and then puttin' them on. You need medical attention now. I've got to get you to the doctor. You'll see the boys when we get there." Caleb gently lifts her and carries her to the car. She clings to him, her face in his shoulder, trying to hide her nakedness and shame. When they reach the car he wraps her in the blanket, sits her on the front seat where she will be next to him and he speeds off to Dr. Marshall's office.

"Do you feel like talkin' Josette? It's ok if you don't want to right now. I understand."

"It was the Spinner brothers Caleb. They took us by surprise. We couldn't get away. Stevie hit one of them in the nose with a rock. He was so brave." Josette starts to cry again.

"That Stevie is a feisty kid. Dr. Marshall is takin' good care of them. They'll be fine. When I find those no good Spinners, nothin' will ever be fine with them again. As soon as I'm sure you're gonna be ok, I'm gonna go see Lloyd and we'll make them pay legally for what they did. It's a good thing I was a Sheriff at one time and respect the law, otherwise I would hunt them down and kill them."

"Don't count on the law Caleb. You're not the sheriff any more and you know how the law works when it comes to a conflict between colored and white people."

"You leave that up to me Sweetheart. I'll make it work."

Chapter 29

Dr. Marshall assures Caleb that Josette and the boys will be fine. The beatings they took are not life threatening. The worse injury is Timmy's broken arm and that will heal with no after effects. He tells Caleb, "I've sent for the boys' mother. She'll be here soon. I know you're not the sheriff anymore Caleb but I would like to know if these men are going to be arrested." Dr. Marshall is furious. "Nobody should be allowed to get away with beating children this way. Their grandmother's beating could have been worse. She could have been raped too. I wonder why she wasn't."

Caleb is stunned. He assumed Josette was raped because she was tied up and naked. "I don't know why either Dr. Marshall. I'm sure they meant to. Somethin' must have spooked them. They've been after her for years. Did she say anythin'? Does she know they didn't touch her that way?"

"Yes I told her. She'll be fine. I'm going to keep her and the boys here a little while longer but they should be able to go home tonight."

"Thank you Dr. Marshall. I'm on my way to see Lloyd now and I assure you those boys wont get away with this." Caleb leaves the doctor's office and goes to see the Sheriff. Lloyd is at his desk when he gets there. He tells Lloyd what the Spinners did to Josette and her grandsons. "Do you know where they are or where they hang out?"

Lloyd is disturbed. Caleb is too upset. He has never seen him in this state before. "Don't worry Caleb we'll find them. They're too stupid to run."

"Lloyd, I want you to deputize me so I can help find them."

"O k Caleb, but we take them alive. No revenge, ok? We have to question them first. Then we'll decide what to do."

"Stop worryin' Lloyd. I may be retired but I'm still a lawman. I'm not about to go against the law now but those boys are gonna pay and it's gonna be legal."

Lloyd is convinced, "Ok Caleb, let's go. We'll try their home first. They just might be stupid enough to go home."

Mr. and Mrs. Spinner are sitting on the front porch when the Sheriff pulls into the driveway. Mr. Spinner gets out of his chair and meets Lloyd at the steps.

Mary Spinner says, "Henry, that's the Sheriff's car. Oh Lord, what did they do now!"

While Lloyd talks to the Spinners, Caleb hangs back and looks around.

"Evenin' folks, I'm lookin' for your boys. Are they home?"

Henry Spinner has heard these word many times before. "No Sheriff, I ain't seen them since early this mornin'. What have they done now?"

"Well this time it's a little more serious. They beat up a grandmother and her two grandsons; two little boys not able to fight grown men. This time they goin' away for a long time. Do you mind if we look around?"

Mrs. Spinner starts to cry. Henry Spinner goes to his wife to comfort her.

"Go ahead sheriff, look all you want. They live mostly in the cellar. I hope you catch them. I'm tired of them bringin' shame to my house."

Lloyd and Caleb search the house from top to bottom. There's no sign of the Spinner boys.

On the way back to the office Caleb says, "Lloyd, I think those boys are stupid enough to return home. They don't work so they have no money. Josette was able to stay out of their way for many years. I think they came on her and the boys accidentally and took advantage of what they thought of as good luck. They're not far. I'm gonna stake out the house all night. I bet they come back."

"Ok Caleb, meanwhile, I'll look around town and put the word out that I want them for questionin'. Somebody will turn them in. I don't know one person in this town who likes those boys. One more thing Caleb, I know you still have your gun. Are you carryin'?"

No Lloyd, my gun is at home. I don't need one for these two. I promise they'll pay legally."

Caleb is right about the Spinners. They have no plan. They have no money and they thought there would be no consequences for what they did. Who would believe a colored's word against a white man? Evidently these stupid brothers are unaware that their own people hate them. Maybe they would be right about nobody believing a colored's word, except for one thing. Both good people and bigots don't like to see children hurt. It makes them angry.

Hecky and Boots are hiding out in the woods in back of their parents home waiting for dark. The only plan they had was to sneak in the house after their parents went to sleep, change clothes and get some sleep too.

While Caleb is waiting and watching, Henry and Mary Spinner are in bed talking.

"Mary, this is the last straw. The sheriff is lookin' for them again. I've made up my mind about somethin'. I hope you agree. Let's sell the house and move away, now. Let's go away someplace where no body knows us. Maybe we can travel a bit. We ain't been no where. It's time we enjoyed the rest of our days. God didn't say we could have tomorrow. Think on it Mary; this may be our last chance to have a little fun. Those boys bought us nothin' but trouble since they was born. Let's sell this house and spend every penny on us. I don't want to leave them nothin'."

Mary is quiet while her husband is speaking. She agreed with almost everything he said. "They was a joy when they was babies Henry. Remember how much fun we had with them? They changed after they started school and they got worse every year. This ain't the first time the Sheriff come here lookin' for them but this time I got a bad feelin'. Did they do somethin' real bad? If they did, maybe they will keep them for a long time. Then, by the time they get out of jail we'll be long gone. Yes Henry, sell the house. I'm tired of people feelin' sorry for us and lookin' at us like it's our fault them boys turned out so bad."

Henry leans over and kisses his wife. "I knew you wouldn't let me down Mary. I'll start cleanin' out the cellar tomorrow. We can't show this house to anybody the way that cellar looks now."

That night Henry and Mary go to sleep hugging each other. They each have pleasant dreams about traveling and having fun. They're night is peaceful until the hours just before dawn. They're awakened by their sons screaming as Lloyd and Caleb drag them out of the cellar in handcuffs.

Chapter 30

No one has seen the Spinner Brothers. Lloyd asked questions all over town. He even questioned the whores the Spinners sometimes saw. Even the whores hated the Spinner Brothers. Lloyd waited until after dark to drive out to where Caleb is watching the Spinner's home. He tells Caleb, "Nobody's seen those boys, Caleb. I asked everywhere. How long are you gonna stay out here?"

"I'll be here till mornin' Lloyd. I'm sure they'll show. They're too stupid not to."

"Ok Caleb, I'm goin' back to the office. I'll be there all night. I'll come check on you every two hours. When they come home, wait for me. We'll take them together. It'll be easier that way."

"Sure Lloyd, as long as they stay in the house, I'll wait, but if they try to leave, they're mine. I'll bring them in and I promise, I'll bring them in alive." Caleb stays in the car watching until midnight. He watched as the lights go out downstairs and a light goes on upstairs. He can see movement behind closed shades. He assumes Mr. and Mrs. Spinner are preparing to retire for the night. Then all the lights go out and the house is dark. Caleb waits. Around midnight he quietly leaves his car and walks in the shadows around the house. He observes every door and window to familiarize himself with the layout of the house. There are two doors; one in the front and one in the back. The windows on the first floor can be easily gotten into without a ladder. The basement windows are too small for a man to get into but large enough for plenty of light and air. Two basement windows are in the front and can be seen from the street. If a light is turned on in the basement, Caleb will know it. Satisfied that he knows this house, he goes back to his car to wait some more. Lloyd arrives right on schedule, soon after midnight.

"Hey Caleb, everythin' all right?"

"Yeah, the old folks went to bed and I checked the house; nothin' yet."

"The town is pretty quiet tonight, so when I come back, I'll stay. See you in two hours. Remember Caleb, wait for me."

Caleb can't help smiling. He knows Lloyd is worried about him. He has no intention of letting Lloyd down. Caleb is calm now so he truthfully tells Lloyd he'll wait. "Ok Lloyd, see you when you get back." Earlier, if those boys had shown up before he got his emotions under control he's not sure what he would have done. Visions of Josette on the ground naked kept flashing through his mind. He had to get control before the Spinners showed up. It took a while. Lloyd coming by every two hours helped. Caleb has traded blind uncontrolled anger for cold calculated fury. Those boys will never know they escaped death to go to jail.

Lloyd returns around three in the morning and joins Caleb in his car to wait. "I hope you're right about those boys Caleb. It'll be light soon."

"Don't worry Lloyd, they'll show. Thanks for comin' back. I could handle those boys by myself but I needed company to keep my mind off Josette."

They settle in and no longer talk. The car is quiet as the remaining night hours creep by. Just before dawn a light goes on in the basement. Both men see it at the same time. They leave the car and approach the back door from opposite directions. The back door is not locked. They quietly enter the kitchen. To the left is the door leading to the basement. Lloyd has his gun drawn. They ease the door open and quietly go down to a room at the bottom of the stairs. It's empty but they can hear water running and someone moving around in the next room. Hecky is standing there with his back to Lloyd and Caleb. He only has on a pair of underwear. He's holding a pair of pants to put on when Caleb says, "You won't need those pants boy. Put them down!"

Hecky spins around to see a gun pointed at his face. He yells, "Don't shoot, don't shoot! I ain't done nothin'!"

"Get down on the floor, now! Put your hands behind your back!"

Hecky is scared and does as Caleb tells him. Caleb handcuffs him and tells him to be quiet. They can hear water running in the bathroom. Lloyd and Caleb position themselves on each side of the bathroom door. Caleb tells Hecky, "Call your brother to come out, now!"

"Ok Sheriff, ok. Hey Boots, come here."

Boots doesn't answer. Lloyd kicks Hecky in the leg. "Call him louder."

This time Hecky yells loud enough to wake his parents. "Boots, hey Boots come here!"

Boots comes out of the bathroom naked with a washcloth in his hand.

"What you want Hecky?" He screams when a gun is pushed under his nose.

"Get on the floor!" Lloyd is on Boots immediately and handcuffs him. Lloyd laughs. "This was easier than I thought it would be. I'm sure glad you were right, Caleb. Ok boys on your feet. You're goin' to jail."

Hecky says, "Wait Sheriff, we ain't got no clothes on. Can't we get dressed?"

Caleb answers him with a sneer. "You got on all you need. Boots, where are your draws?"

"In the bathroom Sheriff, but I can't put them on with these cuffs on my hands." Caleb goes in the bathroom and gets Boot's underwear, brings it out to him and says, "Open your mouth wide." When he doesn't move fast enough, Caleb grabs his nose and pulls his head back. Boots screams in pain, and Caleb jams his draws in his mouth. "When you get to jail you can put them on. If you open your mouth and drop them, you'll go without. Now, both of you get up those stairs!"

By the time they get Hecky and Boots up the stairs into the kitchen, Mr. and Mrs. Spinner have come down to see what all the noise is about. They watch without saying a word as Lloyd and Caleb drag their sons out of the house.

Hecky is yelling, "Ma, Pa, help us we didn't do nothin'! They makin' a mistake!"

Boots didn't dare yell. He wanted to keep his draws. He kept his teeth tightly clenched against them.

The boys are separated when they get to the cars. One goes in the car with Caleb and the other goes in the police car with Lloyd.

Caleb tells Lloyd, "Make him get on the floor on his knees with his head down behind the driver's seat. Keep your night stick on the seat next to you. That way if he tries to get up, you can drive and swing your arm back and hit him in the ass at the same time."

Lloyd is laughing. "You never taught me that one Caleb."

It's called ball control. If his head was the other way, when he tried to get up you could only hit him in the head. Most men don't mind gettin' hit in the head but if they think you might hit them in the balls they get scared. That really scares them."

Lloyd has learned another trick to controlling a prisoner and he laughs all the way back to the station. Secretly, he wishes Hecky would try something so he could try out Caleb's strategy. When they get to the station, Lloyd deliberately puts them in the same cell they were in before. The same cell where Hecky almost died. He tells them, "Don't give me any trouble boys. Remember what happened the last time you were in this cell? It could happen again." He leaves them to think over what he just said.

Boots has put his underwear on and wrapped himself in the threadbare blanket on his cot. Hecky sits there glaring at Lloyd and says nothing. Lloyd leaves them alone.

Back in the office he and Caleb talk about these two stupid men.

Lloyd asks, "When do you think we should charge them?"

"Not yet. Let them stew for a while. They might get nervous if we don't charge them right away. I'm goin' over to see how Josette and the boys are. I'll be back soon. We'll question them then. I hope you understand I'm not steppin' on your toes, Lloyd. I know how to handle people like them. I've had more experience dealin 'with that kind of trash but if you want me to back off just say so. I won't mind."

"No Caleb, I don't mind. I'm still learnin' from you. I appreciate any advice you give me. You go on and see your friend. I'll wait until you come back."

"Thanks Lloyd, we'll question them together. I won't be long."

Meanwhile the Spinner Brothers are feeling insecure with no clothes on. Boots is still wrapped in his blanket. "What they waitin' for Hecky? They just left us here. I'm gettin' scared. Is Lloyd gonna beat us again?"

"I don't know Boots. I think they makin' us wait on purpose. They didn't say why they jailed us. We wasn't drunk. We'll find out soon. Don't let them know you're sacred. Maybe that's what they want. Go to sleep. We were up all night in the woods. Let's get some sleep while we can."

Chapter 31

Caleb goes to see Doctor Marshall. "Good mornin' Doctor. I come to see how Josette and the boys are."

"Good Morning Sheriff Carter, medically they're fine. Cathy took them home yesterday. Timmy was hurt more than his brother. He has a broken arm but children heal quickly. Did you catch the men who did this?"

"Yeah, we caught them early this mornin'. Don't worry. I'll make sure they pay for what they did. Thank you for takin' care of Josette and the boys and don't forget, send me the bill. I'll take care of it. Dr. Marshall, call me Caleb. I'm not the sheriff anymore."

"I know but I've known you as Sheriff Carter all these years. It will take some doing to change a habit and don't you worry about Josette and the boys. In time they'll be as healthy as they were before. I plan to see them again in a few days."

Caleb leaves Dr. Marshall's office and goes to Cathy's house to see Josette. He's a little worried about Cathy's attitude towards him. He hopes she doesn't blame him for what happened to her mother and her children.

Cathy opens the door. He can see she has been crying. "Good mornin' Cathy. I'd like to see Josette and the boys. Dr. Marshall said they're gonna be fine. I'm so sorry I wasn't there, Cathy. I could have prevented this. I was only gone for a couple hours." The look on Cathy's face brings tears to his eyes. This emotion of guilt and fear at the same time is something new to him. Caleb stands there not knowing what to do.

Suddenly Cathy is crying and hugging Caleb. Through her tears she says, "I'm sorry I was mean to you Caleb. Dr. Marshall told me what you did for my children and my mother. Thank you, thank you I'll never act like that again to anyone. It was so unfair of me to treat you that way."

Caleb hugs Cathy and says, "It's all right Cathy. I love your mother and your boys. There's nothin' I wouldn't do for them. I love those boys like they were my own grandchildren. It's over. The

Spinners are in jail and this time they'll be there for a long time. By the time they get out your boys will be grown. I don't think they'll bother any one again."

"Thank you for being so understanding. Come on, I'll take you to see Momma. The boys have been asking for you too. You're their hero. They can't wait to see you."

"I'd like to see the boys first. I don't think Josette will mind."

"Sure, come on. Hey boys, look who's here. I'll tell Mommy you're here, Caleb."

Stevie and Timmy are in bed. When Caleb comes in the room they both yell, "Hey Mr. Carter!"

"Hey, are you two ok? You look good."

Stevie says, "We're fine. Did you catch those bad Spinners?"

"Yes Stevie, we got them. They're in jail and they won't be botherin' any one again. I'm sorry I didn't get back in time. I could have stopped them from hurtin' you."

"It's ok Mr. Carter. You took us to Dr. Marshall and you found Grandma. You helped us and do you know what's even better?"

"No Stevie, what's better? what are you talkin' about?"

"Now, Mommy likes you too. I thought she hated you but not now. She likes you Mr. Carter. She likes you like we do!"

"That's great Stevie. You boys rest now. I'm gonna go see Grandma. Timmy are you all right?"

"Yes but my arm hurts. He broke my arm." Timmy starts to cry.

"I know Timmy, but he's in jail now and that's where he's gonna stay. He won't hurt anybody else again. I'll be back to see you tomorrow."

"Ok Mr. Carter, see you tomorrow." Timmy cheers up and says goodbye with a smile.

Caleb leaves the boys feeling better now that he has seen how well they're doing physically and mentally. He was afraid the fear of some one hurting them again could take away the joy of being a child. There's nothing worse than a fearful child but these two boys seem to have an indomitable spirit.

Now, he's anxious to see Josette. She's sitting on the couch in the living room and calls him when he comes out of the boy's room. "I'm here Caleb." She has a big smile on her face. I'm so glad to see you."

"Well, look at you. I expected to find you in bed. Are you feelin' ok?" Caleb kisses Josette's hands and sits next to her on the couch.

"I'm fine Caleb, thank you for taking care of my boys. What about the Spinners have you caught them yet?"

"Yes, they're in jail now. Lloyd is waitin' for me to get back. We're gonna question them together. We'll make sure those two get put away for a long time. They don't belong around decent people. One thing puzzles me Josette. Those boys been stalkin' you for years, yet when they finally get you, they don't do what they planned all those years. I wonder why."

"You can't say it can you Caleb? You were afraid they had raped me."

"I was Sweetheart, but Dr. Marshall told me that didn't happen. I'm thankful you were saved that. No Josette, I can't say that word. Not when it comes to you. I might have killed them on the spot. Then I would be just as bad as they are."

"If they had raped me Caleb, would that make a difference in how you feel about me?"

"Oh no Josette!" That's not what I meant. Nothin' in this world could make me change how I feel about you. Please say you believe me." Caleb is visibly upset.

"I do believe you Caleb. I'm sorry I sounded doubtful. They didn't rape me because of what I said. Hecky was on top of me showing rotten teeth and stinking when I told him I was white. You should have seen the look on his face. He was horrified. You should have seen him scrambling to get off me. It seems, it's ok to rape a colored woman but it's repulsive to have sex with a white woman after she has been with a colored man. He said I was spoiled. No white man would ever want me again. I was spoiled for good white men. He called himself good, Caleb. He called himself good! He was so angry. He started to beat me when I laughed. Josette hugs Caleb and starts to cry. "Caleb, why are people so rotten? Why is the South so hateful? Colored women are always in danger. Our children aren't

119

safe. You and I can't be together and be happy. Strangers who don't even know us hate us. The South is a bad place for people like us Caleb. What are we going to do? Why is this place such a hell to live in?"

"Don't cry Josette. You're at a low place now and feelin' sorry for yourself. Tomorrow will be a better day. Nobody's gonna keep us from bein' happy Sweetheart, I promise."

They sit quietly for a while. Then Josette says, "I've got a lot of thinking to do Caleb. You go back to that jail and make sure those boys pay for what they did. Come back tomorrow to see me and I'll tell you what I have decided to do."

"Ok Sweetheart, while you're thinkin' you think about us. I'll always be here. You remember I love you no matter what. I ain't goin' away so don't think about leavin' me!" Caleb's mind is at ease as he leaves Josette sitting on the couch. He doesn't know what she has to think about that's so important and he refuses to believe it's something bad.

Chapter 32

Lloyd is at his desk when Caleb walks in. "You been gone a long time Caleb. Is everythin' ok with Josette?"

"Physically she's fine but I'm worried about her emotionally. We have to keep these boys in jail. Let's go question them."

The Spinner brothers are asleep. Lloyd and Caleb watch them for a few minutes. Caleb's anger starts to rise. "Look at them sleepin' like they don't have a care in the world. They cause innocent people pain then act as if nothin' happened. Wake them up Lloyd."

Lloyd takes his nightstick and hits the bars as hard as he can. "Wake up boys! We got somethin' to talk about!"

Instantly the Spinners sit up. Boots is terrified and backs up in the corner of his bed. He remembers the last beating he took from Sheriff Lloyd. Hecky is defiant. He's scared too but won't let it show.

"What do you want Sheriff? When we gettin' out of here? We ain't drunk."

Caleb speaks first. "We want to be fair to you boys so tell us why you beat up two little boys and raped their grandmother."

Hecky yells at Caleb but his eyes never leave Lloyd. Lloyd has his nightstick in one hand and uses it to hit the palm of his other hand. The smacking sound makes Hecky nervous. "We didn't rape nobody Sheriff! We don't mess with nigger women!"

Boots speaks up before Hecky can shut him up. "I thought you said she wasn't colored Hecky."

"Shut up Boots!"

Caleb is smiling to himself as Hecky incriminates himself. "Ok Hecky tell us about those little boys. You're a big man. Why beat up two children? One of them is hurt bad."

"That was Boots. I didn't touch them pickaninnies."

Boots speaks up in his own defense. "I only hit them because one of them threw a rock and hit Hecky in the nose."

"Well it don't matter now. You're goin' to jail for a long time because you were protectin' your big bad brother from two little boys."

Hecky is still Defiant. "Oh yeah? Who's gonna believe a nigger woman and two pickaninnies over a white man? You might as well let us out now. We ain't goin' to jail for nothin' like that."

Caleb is openly smiling now. "We'll see boys. Come on Lloyd we've got work to do. We'll be back soon boys. Get your stories straight. You'll need a good one."

Lloyd and Caleb go back to the office and sit a while without saying anything. They're both thinking about a lawful way of making the Spinners pay for what they did. Finally Lloyd speaks up. "Caleb, those boys might be right. Can we take a chance on a trial with only white folks on the jury?"

"I know Lloyd. No, we can't take a chance on a trial. You never know how people will act. There's a lot of ignorant people in this town. If a few of them get on a jury and their lawyer spouts a lot of garbage, those boys could get off. It doesn't matter what the evidence says. The only chance we have of keepin' them in jail is to get them to sign a confession."

"A confession! Caleb, if you think you're gonna get them to do that you're crazy. Boots might be that stupid but Hecky ain't."

"Don't be too sure Lloyd. I've got a plan I've been sittin' here thinkin'. Josette told me somethin' today I had forgotten about. It's an ugly superstition folks used to believe. Let's wait a while then go back in and question them again. We'll give them time to worry some more. When we go back I'll do all the talkin'. You follow my lead. You'll understand. I'm gonna write out a confession for them and when I get through with them, they'll sign it."

Lloyd wonders what Caleb is up to but he doesn't question him. One thing he does know, Caleb Carter is a whole lot smarter than Hecky and Boots Spinner.

It takes Caleb thirty minutes to finish writing out the confession and another thirty minutes to correct and edit the language to suit him. His hunt and peck method of typing takes another thirty minutes to finish the confession. Finally it's done and he says, "Ok Lloyd, it's time. Let's go see the Spinners."

This time the Spinners are awake but when Lloyd hits the bars with his nightstick both of them jump. The scare tactic works again. They think Lloyd is there to beat them.

Caleb smiles to see the fear on their faces. "Ok boys we're gonna make you a deal. If you take it, your jail time won't be long and you can go home. I wrote out a confession for you to sign."

Hecky jumps up and yells, "Are you crazy? We ain't signin' no confession!"

"Hold on boy! Wait just a minute. You might like what you hear. I'm not finished. The charge against you is beatin' up two children and rapin' a white woman. We could reduce the charge to three counts of assault. If you sign this confession you won't have to go to trial. The judge won't give you as much time because he'll believe you co-operated with us. You been in jail before. You know what it's like."

Boots jumps up off the bed and runs over to his brother. "Sign it Hecky! I don't want to go to jail no more. You know what they do to me every time. They used me like a woman Hecky! I ain't no woman. Please Hecky, I don't want to go to jail."

Hecky is upset too. "Calm down Boots, let me finish talkin' to the sheriff. Wait a minute Sheriff. What white woman you talkin' about. We didn't rape no white woman. You can't put us on trial for that."

"Oh yes we can. You thought that woman you been chasin' all these years was colored. You thought because she was colored you could do anythin' you wanted to her and get away with it. Well, maybe that would be true, if she was colored. I've got news for you Hecky. She really is white!" Caleb emphasized these last words by shouting.

Hecky is stunned but doesn't say anything.

Caleb continues. "She's been passin' for colored all these years and she says you raped her. If we go to trial, we have to pick a jury. How many friends do you have in this town? How many people have you stole from? How many jobs have you been fired from? Do you think we'll be able to find twelve people who will believe you? Now get this through that thick head of yours. The District Attorney will stack that jury with as many white women as he can. No matter what this woman did in her life she's still white and I'm gonna marry her!

My word carries a lot of weight in this town. Do you want to take a chance on twelve people who hate you settin' you free or do you want to take a chance on one judge who might go easy on you because you signed a confession. One more thing, there's a lot of good white people in this town. Some of them will be on that jury and no matter what the racial relations are, I'll bet not one of those women on the jury will like the idea of you beatin' up little boys and breakin' one of their arms. They'll think about their own children and be afraid you might do the same thing again and next time it might be one of their own. If you go to trial, you'll go to jail for a long time. If you confess, you might get thirty days for each offense. Take it or leave it now! I'm not waitin' one minute more!" These last few words scare the Spinners because of the way Caleb said it. The threat was real and the Spinners felt it.

Hecky's defiance is gone. "Ok Sheriff ok!. We'll sign. We didn't know she was white."

"Yes you did you lyin' piece of dirt. She told you she was white!" Caleb is disgusted and is beginning to lose his temper. He hands Lloyd the confession.

"Here Lloyd have them sign it. I'll see you later."

"Ok boys, come over here one at a time. Hecky, you sign first."

Hecky signs the confession without reading it. Then asks Lloyd, "Can we get some clothes? It's cold, we been like this all night."

Lloyd ignores Hecky's request. "Ok Boots you're next. Sign right here."

Boots signs then asks Hecky, "Ask him can we get somethin' to eat too. I'm hungry. We ain't had nothing to eat since yesterday mornin'."

Lloyd laughs at them. "How does it feel boys being naked and hungry? I'll get you somethin' in a little while." He leaves the Spinners sitting on their cots wrapped in their blankets. He goes to the office and sits in his chair thinking about what just happened. He's pleased the Spinner brothers will get what they deserve. Then he reads the confession. Caleb has tricked them. There is nothing in the confession about a reduced charge. Everything they did to Josette and her grandchildren is spelled out in detail but there is no mention of rape. Lloyd is disturbed and worried about Caleb. Why did he leave out rape? Those boys would get more time if rape was included whether it was done or not. He could have said attempted rape. I'll ask him when I see him. He must really be upset for him to do this. Caleb has always been a champion of the law even though some prisoners did occasionally get jailhouse whippings; he had never done anything this serious before. Lloyd doesn't know if this confession is unethical, unlawful or both. Those boys deserve what they will get because of that confession but will it be true justice? Lloyd doesn't know.

Chapter 33

The confession is signed. Caleb breathes a sigh of relief. The charges against the Spinner brothers are kidnapping and assault of a grandmother and her two grandchildren. Nowhere in the confession is race mentioned and Caleb is sure the Spinners won't open their mouths since he omitted the rape charge. If it should come up, Caleb is sure his testimony will out weigh anything the Spinners have to say. Their previous criminal record should convince the judge they belong in jail for a long time. By the time they get out, Timmy and Stevie will be teenagers and almost grown. The Spinner brothers are cowards and Caleb is sure they wouldn't try anything on someone their own size. Caleb is exhausted but his mind is at ease. Josette and the boys are doing fine and the threat she has been living under for so many years is over. He tells Lloyd he's going home to get some sleep. He's extremely tired and he thinks sleep will come easy. He's wrong. He tossed and turned unable to close his eyes for more than a few minutes. Images of Josette naked on the ground with her hands and feet tied with belts, kept appearing in his mind. The possibility of what could have happened keeps him tense. She might have been killed and he would have lost her forever. This thought hits him so hard he can hardly breathe. He sits up quickly trying to catch his breath. After a few minutes the panic subsides. It will be a while before he's able to sleep so he leaves his bedroom and goes to sit in the living room. He tells himself he'll go back to bed in a few minutes.

Lloyd comes home around midnight and finds him asleep on the couch.

When Caleb wakes early the next morning. He has a pillow under his head and a blanket over him. Lloyd enters the room with a cup of coffee.

"Here old man, drink this. You were dead to the world when I came in last night. How are you feelin' this mornin'?"

"I'm fine Lloyd. Thanks for coverin' me up. Yesterday was rough for everybody. I'm glad it's over."

Lloyd sits down in one of the very comfortable chairs they have in their living room with his cup of coffee. He's quiet for a few seconds then he says, "Caleb, I'm worried about somethin'. I read that confession. You told those boys they would get a reduced charge if they signed it. What's the reduced charge? You put in everything except rape or attempted rape."

"You have to read between the lines Lloyd. The reduced charge is leavin' out the attempted rape. Includin' it would introduce race in this mess. Everyone in this town knows Josette is not white, except those stupid Spinner boys. I didn't want to take a chance on a judge or possibly a jury would have that same ugly superstition the Spinners have. That would have ruined everythin'. If we don't charge them their lawyer can't bring it up. The most important charge is kidnappin'. That's what's goin' to keep them in jail for a long time. If Hecky finally understands what happened and starts to rant and rave about Josette's race, the judge or a jury, if there is one, will think he's tryin' to get away with what he did. The confession should avoid havin' to pick a jury. Don't worry Lloyd I did nothin' illegal."

Lloyd breathes a sigh of relief. "Thanks Caleb, for explainin' that. I was worried."

"I'm glad you talked it over with me Lloyd."

Caleb plans to see Reverend Roberts. He needs someone to talk to. Time has no importance to him this morning so he doesn't realize it's seven o'clock when he knocks on the Reverend's door. Reverend Roberts is up but not prepared for visitors. He opens the door in his bathrobe.

"Caleb, what's the matter? Come in son. You don't look so good." He takes Caleb's arm and leads him to a chair in the kitchen. Join me in a cup of coffee. I just made it."

"Thanks Reverend. I need to talk to you. You've always helped me in the past. I need you to assure me we're not already in hell. You don't have to die to go to hell Reverend. I've been dealin' with evil all my life but this is the first time I really feel what it's like."

"Caleb, you have always given me some interesting things to think about and pray about. Tell me, what has you so upset."

"For the first time in my life I'm in love and I almost lost her. I almost lost her to ignorance and hate. Caleb is close to tears and has to stop talking until he gets control. Reverend Roberts waits patiently. When Caleb starts to talk again, he tells the Reverend how he met Josette and her grandchildren. He tells the funny story about dancing with the turtle. He tells about the happy times they spent at the lake. Then he tells Reverend Roberts, Josette is colored and watches his expression carefully. He detects no surprise or negative response in the Reverend to this information so he continues to talk. When he gets to the Spinner Brothers, he has to stop at times to calm down the anger he feels building up in his gut.

Reverend Roberts quietly waits and prays for Caleb. At the end of the story Caleb says, "That's why I'm so upset Reverend. I came real close to killin' those boys. I never felt that rage before. It scared me. It made me wonder if we're already in hell."

"As usual Caleb, you have presented me with an interesting question. This time I can answer you positively and I pray it helps. We're not living in hell, Caleb. There is no redemption in hell. Even though there is evil all around us, God is alive and well. His grace and mercy endures. Good happens all the time. God's miracles happen all the time. Unfortunately we hear about the evil more than we do the good. Satan gives himself a lot of press. The religious community refuses to advertise his evil deeds. We rejoice in God's miracles and love and we help those Satan harms without calling his name. We give him no press. This is God's world Caleb. All of us have the opportunity to be redeemed. It's our choice. You don't have a choice in hell. That's the last stop. You're a good man Caleb. In your job you've had to deal with a lot of evil and it has not changed you. Be at ease Caleb. Your friend and her grandchildren survived. That was God. It was another triumph over evil. I hope I've been a help to you Caleb. I'll continue to pray for you. Goodness is the future. It's all around us."

"Thank you Reverend, I do feel better. You're wrong about one thing though. I have changed and I need to pray and ask forgiveness for myself. Before this happened I was a happy man. Listenin' to you makes me believe I can be that way again." He gets ready to leave and says, "I'll be seein' you Reverend, thanks again." Caleb leaves Reverend Roberts with a lighter heart and goes to see Josette.

Chapter 34

Stevie and Timmy are playing in the yard when Caleb gets there. They run to meet him. Timmy has his bubbling personality back.

"Hi Mr. Carter."

"Hi Timmy, Stevie, I see you boys are feelin' better today. How's Grandma?"

Stevie says, "She's fine too Mr. Carter. She's waiting for you."

"Ok boys, I'll see you later. Timmy be careful don't hurt your arm."

"I won't. Mr. Carter It feels better now."

Josette hears them talking and comes to the door. Caleb is coming up the steps. "Good morning Caleb."

"Good mornin' Sweetheart. It's good to see those two playin' again. Kids bounce back quick. How about you?"

"I'm fine too. Come in."

In the hall Caleb hugs Josette. "Are you sure you're ok? Those boys are gonna stay in jail. They won't be out for a very long time. You won't have to worry about them ever again."

"That's good Caleb but let's not talk about them anymore. I've erased them from my mind. I'm too happy right now. Come sit with me. I have something I want to tell you." She takes his hand and leads him to the couch. Her words surprise him. "I want to marry you right away. Let's not wait. I've done a lot of thinking Caleb. We deserve to be happy and we can't let anyone interfere with that. No matter what Lloyd thinks, no matter what my children think or this town thinks; we have the right to be happy and be together for the rest of our lives. My children are grown and have their own lives. Lloyd is grown and has a good career thanks to you."

"I thought you would never stop talkin'. You don't have to convince me. Sweetheart, I've been waitin' for you." Caleb is smiling as he says, "Are you sure Josette, are you sure?"

"Yes Caleb I'm sure. We can have a party at my house and announce our plans. We'll only invite our family and closest friends.

The ones who love us will be happy for us. Others don't matter. Is that ok with you?"

Caleb's smile gets wider. He holds Josette on his lap and they hug each other for a few minutes in silence. At this moment Caleb is the happiest man in the world. Then he says, "Josette, let's hold off for a little while."

Josette is stunned and tries to get up. "Caleb, you are the one who wanted to get married right away! What's going on? Have you changed your mind?"

"No, no Sweetheart, you didn't let me finish. I was tryin' to say, let's hurry and fix up the house at the lake and get married there. We'll have a party to announce our engagement and the weddin'. It will be a surprise for everyone. But, the first thing I have to do is buy you an engagement ring."

Josette feels bad. She has not doubted Caleb before. Why now? "I'm sorry Caleb. That's a wonderful idea but I'm not going shopping for what we need with my face looking like this. Dr. Marshall said it will take at least three weeks for these bruises to disappear. You have to do the shopping alone. We can decide the colors for the house together but the rest is up to you. You will also have to shop for our rings alone."

"No problem Sweetheart. We already decided to keep the house as close to the original as possible. Remember?" I'll take care of gettin' someone to paint and landscape the place. By the time that's finished, you will be well enough to shop for furniture. I can wait a short while to be happy for the rest of my life."

"Me too Caleb, when will you start?"

"When I leave here, I'm goin' straight to the lake. I'll scrape off some paint chips then go to the paint store and match the color. Then, I'll hire a painter to do the job. I know some good men. I know one landscaper who will do a good job. I'm not very good at yard work."

Josette is getting excited. "Caleb, don't let the landscaper touch the flowers growing up the porch and make sure he keeps the grounds as natural as possible. I want lots of flowers growing everywhere."

"Slow down Sweetheart, by the time we get to the landscaper you will be well enough to supervise. Then you can tell him exactly what you want. You'll make it beautiful enough for our weddin' and reception. I can't wait. We've got so much to look forward to."

"We have Caleb. Now, you go get started. This month is going to fly by."

Chapter 35

The next day Caleb gets ready to shop for what he'll need to update the house at the lake. While sitting at the kitchen table, he makes two lists; one for the people who will paint and landscape and one for the supplies he'll need. The list of supplies is easy but who will use them throws him into a quandary. He knows several good painters both white and colored but questions keep running through his mind. Will Josette be offended if he hired all white painters? If he hired both white and colored will they get along or will there be friction between the two. He Doesn't address the issue of who will be in charge because he thinks it will be him. He knows white men won't work for a colored boss and the best painter he knows is Ezra Jamison from Willow Park. Ezra has two steady employees. Both of these men are perfectionists just like their boss. Caleb is getting annoyed thinking about these problems. He talks to himself. "Why the hell do I have to think about the color of a man in every thing I choose to do? This is givin' me a headache. Before I met Josette, I never had to think about these things. Now every minute of my life is consumed with color." Caleb is getting discouraged. He leaves the lists on the table and goes to the front porch and sits on the glider Josette likes so much. Sitting there, He remembers her words. "Will you be strong enough to stand up to the everyday pressures of loving a colored woman? It won't be easy Caleb. You're going to be tested." The first test is upon him and it comes from within himself, not from others. He has to make a decision. One he thought would be simple until he started to think about the social problems of the south. He tells himself, "Ok Caleb, make up your mind and stick to it. Make it work, even if you have to be there every minute of every day the work is goin' on." Caleb is determined there will be no unpleasantness at a place where he plans to be happy with the woman he loves. This thought frees his mind. He makes his decision. Ezra Jamison will get the job of painting the house. "I'll go see him this afternoon." He breathes a sigh of relief. All that confused thinking is what gave him his headache. Now he has to think about the landscaper. He only knows one. Mitch Allen is white and he only hires colored men to work for him. Caleb never thought about this before. He can feel his headache getting worse. "How the hell do people live like this every day? This is small everyday stuff. Why should it be a possible life changin' situation?" Caleb has made his decision but it took two hours and a headache to accomplish. He knows he can never share what he went through today with Josette. He's afraid it would make her unhappy and possibly make her doubt him. Nothing is going to come between him and the only woman he has ever loved. "The hell with this I'm goin' to the paint store."

At the paint store he picks up several paint charts to show Josette. Then he goes to see Ezra Jamison. Ezra's on a ladder painting his own house when Caleb arrives.

"Good mornin' Ezra. Can you come down a minute and talk? I got a job for you"

"Sure thing Sheriff, what's on your mind?"

"Call me Caleb, Ezra. You know I'm not the sheriff any more."

"Yeah, I know but habit is hard to break. It just comes out without me thinkin'. What can I do for you?"

"I bought a house at Blue Mountain Lake and it needs paintin' Can you do the job?"

"I sure can but I have to see the house before I can give you a price. When can I see it?"

"How about early tomorrow mornin'? I can pick you up at seven."

"That's fine, I'll be ready. I'm sure glad you didn't say now. My wife would be real mad if I left this unfinished. She's been after me for a year to paint our house."

Caleb and Ezra laugh and shake hands. Then Caleb goes to see Mitch Allen. Mitch is working at Mayor Sykes' house.

Caleb calls, "Hey Mitch!"

"Caleb, ain't seen you in a while. How you doin' since you retired?"

"I'm doin' just fine. I got a job for you, if you have the time."

"I'll make time. I'm just finishin' the Mayor's house. I can start yours tomorrow."

"No, tomorrow's too soon. I bought a house at Blue Mountain Lake. The yard's pretty overgrown. I want the place landscaped so it looks good. The grass is high, weeds are everywhere but flowers are still growin' up the porch. I want them left. I won't need you for two weeks. Is that all right?"

"That's fine Caleb but why so long?"

"Ezra Jamison is paintin' the place and I don't want grass blowin' around while the paint is wet. When he's done you can start."

"Ezra's a good man. He's the best painter I've ever seen. He'll do a good job. I still would like to see the place so I can decide what I have to do and what I'm gonna plant."

"Ok with me but the place is hard to find. I'll draw you a map. Go anytime you want to. Show me the plans as soon as you can. I was wonderin' about somethin' Mitch. I noticed over the years you only hire colored men to work for you. Why is that?"

"It's simple Caleb. I can't afford to pay white men what they want and still make a livin' for myself. Coloreds work cheaper and I don't have no trouble out of them. Don't get me wrong Caleb. I pay them fair. I tried to hire both colored and white but it was too much trouble. The white men wanted to boss the coloreds and I'm the boss. I tell everybody what to do. I couldn't make the whites understand that and then the coloreds wouldn't work for me and other white men too. There was just too much friction. It's better this way for everybody, especially me. I still have to be at every job. You would be surprised how my white customers think they can tell my men what to do. Some of the women had them emptying their garbage and cleanin' out their sheds or garages, when they were suppose to be doin' the work I told them to do. I put a stop to that. Now I'm at every job. Sometimes it's a pain but I've got good steady men workin' for me and I don't want to lose them. When I'm there things run smoothly. Do you have any objection to my men workin' on your place?" Mitch's tone of voice changed and surprised Caleb.

"Oh no Mitch, who you have workin' for you is fine with me. I just wondered that's all. I never had to hire anybody before. Lloyd keeps our place in fine shape. You got the job. When you have the plans drawn up come see me."

Mitch's tone of voice returned to being friendly. "Ok Caleb, see you in a couple days."

Mayor Sykes was watching from his front window. After Caleb leaves he comes out to talk to Mitch.

In a sarcastic tone he asks, "What did that Caleb Carter want?"

"Nothin' much Mayor, Just some work done at his house. I'll take care of it for him." Mitch doesn't like the Mayor's way of asking about Caleb. Something about his attitude bothers Mitch. "You got a problem with Caleb, Mayor?"

"No, I'm just glad he's not the sheriff any more. That man has been a thorn in my side for thirty years."

Mitch didn't say anything else but he was thinking; he was a thorn in your side because you're a klansman, you old fart.

Meanwhile Caleb goes to the house at the lake and compares the paint samples with the color of the house. Then he takes them to Josette for her approval. His headache didn't leave him until he saw a smile brighten up her face.

Caleb didn't know his headache was a tension headache but through his life with Josette he will have many more and will come to know them for what they are.

Chapter 36

Three weeks go by fast and Josette is well enough in her own mind to go out in public. She can't wait to see the house at Blue Mountain Lake. Caleb has kept her up on the progress of its restoration but she wants to see for herself. The painting inside and out is finished and the landscaper starts this week. Josette wants to be there when he starts. Caleb has shown her the plans Mitch drew up and it appears he has not touched the flowering vines growing up the porch rails. Josette wants to be sure no one makes a mistake and tears them down.

She questioned why the landscaper had to wait until the painter finished before he could start work. Caleb told her that's the way Ezra wanted it. He said the fewer people who knew he was working at Caleb's house, the better it was for him. Ezra was protecting himself and his men from other painters both colored and white. He had a reputation as an excellent painter to uphold and there had been incidents of sabotaged work that he had to contend with. This made him lose money because he had to repaint and repair the damage done by someone unknown. One time, he entered a bid on a city job that was lower than a white painter and he got the job. However, half way through the job his supplies were stolen and the tires on his truck were flattened. After that, he never entered a bid on any city job. It just wasn't worth the trouble. Another time, Mrs. Van Warren was looking for someone to paint her mansion. One of her friends recommended Ezra, vouched for his reputation and praised his work as an excellent painter. That recommendation is what got him the job. Ezra didn't know a white painter from town was hoping to get that particular job. Trouble again reared its ugly head when someone broke into the Van Warren's mansion and stole some of her jewelry. It was rumored around town that "Ezra's boys" were the thieves. Ezra knew better and suspected the white painter but there was nothing he could do about it.

Mrs. Van Warren assured him she didn't believe the rumor and let him finish the work. But, Ezra felt she looked at him funny from that day on. She also never left the house when he and his men were working there. Before that, she was never home. She was always out doing her charity work.

Josette understands these type of situations and says nothing more. She and Caleb have discussed these unfair practices before. Caleb was relieved. He didn't want to get into a discussion with her about how unfair the south was to colored people. It made him uncomfortable because he knew all southerners were not that way. Thinking about that injustice made him sad because the ones who had no hatred in their hearts helped the status quo by not speaking out. Many were afraid of their neighbors. Ezra and Mitch knew and respected each other and they were aware that both of them were working on Caleb's house. They scheduled their work at different hours to keep down gossip. When Ezra finished, Mitch started and neither mentioned the other.

Josette and Caleb are on their way to see the house and to meet Mitch. Josette is excited. "Caleb, now that the house is all painted, we can shop for furniture. We won't need much and that's something we can do together."

"Ok Sweetheart, but let's hurry. I want to be ready to get married as soon as the landscapers are finished. Mitch said he needs two weeks to finish. Do you think we can buy furniture and get it here by that time?"

"Sure we can Caleb but that's not the issue. We have to plan the party and set the date. It's going to take me longer than two weeks to get ready. The first thing we have to do is make a guest list. We only have a few friends and they're mostly my family and Lloyd. Is there anyone else you would like to invite?"

"Only Reverend Roberts. He has been a good friend to me for many years."

"Well Caleb, it looks like it will be a small party but a wonderful one. Are you as happy as I am?"

"Yes Josette, sometimes I can't believe this is happenin' to me. I never thought I would ever get married. How did I get to be so lucky to find you? Sometimes a fear comes over me and I think this is too good to be true. I keep waitin' for it all to end."

"Oh Caleb, this won't end. We won't let it. We're going to have a wonderful life."

Caleb takes Josette's hand and they ride in silence for a while, each lost in thought. Then Caleb says, "Josette do you think your girls will object to you marryin' me?"

"I don't know Caleb. Cathy's attitude has changed toward you since you saved her boys but I don't know how she will react to our marriage plans. We'll have to wait and see. No matter how she feels Caleb, we're getting married. She loves me. She'll come around. Janet is different. All she wants is for me to be happy. I don't think we will have to worry about them. What about Lloyd? How do you think he'll react?"

"I don't know but it won't change anythin'. I love him like he was my own son and I'll miss him if he doesn't come to the weddin' but it will be his loss and his problem. I won't make it mine. When I think about how he helped me capture the Spinners after they assaulted you and the boys, and how he defended that mother with the little retarded boy from those rotten Spinner brothers, I believe he will wish us well. He has a good heart."

"Well Caleb, it looks like we're going to have a short guest list" That statement starts them laughing and they laugh all the way to the lake.

Chapter 37

They're almost to the house when Caleb says, "Keep your eyes wide open sweetheart. You are in for a treat."

When the house comes onto view, Josette exclaims, "Oh my! Caleb, is that the same house? It gleams in the sunlight. That Ezra is a miracle worker with paint. It's beautiful!"

Caleb takes Josette's hand. "Come inside there's another miracle in there."

They're coming up the front steps on to the porch when Josette yells, "The glider! Oh Caleb, you brought the glider here? Is it the same one from your house?"

"Yes, I thought I would surprise you. Ezra painted it the same color as the shutters and I bought the pillows. Did I do it right?" Josette is so happy she throws her arms around Caleb and hugs him tight. With tears of happiness in her eyes she says, "You did a wonderful job and you are a wonderful man. Thank you Caleb for bringing a special happiness into my life."

They stand there for a few minutes hugging each other before they enter the house.

Josette is like a child with a new toy. She runs from room to room exclaiming "Oh my, oh my." Each room is a masterpiece. Each room has a accent wall and the paint is so beautifully blended that the accent wall and the rest of the room seem to run together. It's hard to tell where one wall stops and another begins. The bathroom is breathtaking. Upon seeing the bathroom Josette is speechless after yelling with joy in all the other rooms. The original blue birds are still there but they are touched up to show their natural beauty. In the background are wispy clouds floating by in a pale blue sky.

Finally her composure returns and she says, "Caleb, we have to be very careful what furniture we put in these rooms. They are visions of loveliness empty. We can't spoil that look."

"I know sweetheart, that's your job." Caleb is in awe of the happiness in his life and whispers. "Thank you God."

Chapter 38

The big day is here. The house is painted and furnished. The yard is beautifully landscaped, the guests have all arrived and the party is in full swing. All of Josette's family is there. Reverend Roberts and Reverend Coles, the minister of Josette's church, are there with their wives. Lloyd hasn't arrived as yet. However, he promised Caleb he would come as soon as he could. He has to work a few hours to make sure the station is covered.

Dinner is served. Caleb has done all the cooking with the exception of the potato salad. No one makes potato salad like Josette. She told Caleb, "I'll make the potato salad. Don't be offended Caleb but white folks just don't get the way potato salad is suppose to taste. Potato salad has a spirit all its own. You have to be in touch with its essence and aroma. It isn't just food. Watch the expression on the faces when the first forkful goes in the mouth. The eyes close, the head goes back and ummmm comes out of the mouth. It's a mouthwatering delight. That's the effect good potato salad has on people."

Caleb laughs. "Josette, I never know when you're foolin' me. It's ok with me. You make the potato salad."

Everyone is having a good time and everyone is wondering what the party is for. Some think it's a house warming for this beautiful place. All the invitation said was, "We're having a party. Please join us." Everyone is in awe of the house. As they go through the rooms, each one excites them more and more. Because of the location of the house at this part of the lake, everyone assumes the house belongs to Caleb. The thought that this could possibly belong to someone colored never enters their heads. This part of the lake is private property and all the owners are white. It's true both coloreds and whites fish together on the other side on the lake and they are friendly to each other but no colored family lives here. They share bait, hooks and sinkers on many occasions but when the day is over they go separate ways with no social interaction.

Dinner is over. Janet and Cathy made chocolate cake and home made ice cream. Everyone is in the living room eating this wonderful dessert. Stevie and Timmy helped make the ice cream. They took turns turning the handle on the ice cream maker. They love home made ice cream and they are rewarded with the dasher when the ice cream is finished. To them this is the best part. Although the ice cream is good in a bowl it tastes much better licking it off fingers that scoop it off the dasher.

It is now time to reveal the reason of the party. Caleb stands up to get everyone's attention. "Ok folks, listen up. I have an announcement. How do you like this house?" Everyone cheered and clapped. "Have you been wonderin' who it belongs to?"

Cathy speaks up, "We thought it was yours Caleb."

"No Cathy, I bought it for your mother."

Everyone gasps at the same time, then silence fills the room. No adult knew what to say but the innocence of a child comes to their rescue.

Stevie speaks first. "You mean this house is Grandma's?"

Caleb didn't expect the silence but he recovers quickly. "Yes Stevie, you and your friends and everyone here can come here any time you want to."

Stevie and Timmy are overjoyed. "Yippee, thanks Mr. Carter. Thanks Grandma!"

Josette stands up and takes Caleb's hand. "That's not all folks. We brought you all here to day because we know you love us and we want to share something very special with you. Caleb and I are getting married and we want all of you to be at our wedding."

Everyone in the room is shocked into silence again. They sit there with their mouths wide open in surprise.

Cathy jumps up. It's obvious to everyone how upset she is. "Mommy! Have you thought this out? Caleb, is this true? Are you sure? You know what it's like in this town. Oh my God, Mommy you're not moving away, are you?" Cathy is close to tears.

"No Cathy, we're not moving away. Don't be so upset. Yes we have thought this through. We deserve to be happy and we love each other. Nothing is going to stop us. Yes, we know how this town is and they will have to adjust. Everyone will have to adjust. In one month we will be married. We have spoken to Reverend Roberts and Reverend Coles. They have agreed to marry us. The wedding will be here in our garden followed by a party. We want all of you here to celebrate with us. Then we are going on a trip around this country and we intend to enjoy ourselves. Then we will come back here to live."

Janet, Josette's more practical daughter, asks, "How are you traveling Mommy? Are you taking the train or are you driving? Where can you stay? You know how it is with hotels. What will you do if someone suspects you're not white? You know how some people can tell the difference, especially in Louisiana. There, a lot of us look like they could be white. I'm worried Mother. Do you have to do this? I don't mean marry Caleb. I trust him with that. I mean traveling around this country where so many people hate us. I'm afraid Mother."

These words add to Cathy's shock. "Mommy, are you saying you're going to pass for white?"

Josette is beginning to get annoyed. Caleb can sense it. He puts his arm around her shoulders to calm her down. "No Cathy, I'm going just as I am. I'm going to travel this country of ours just like it belongs to me. Just like every other American in it. We're not visitors here Cathy. This is our home. We're here to stay and Caleb and I are going to see as much of it as our money will allow. I refuse to let anyone interfere with my life and take my freedom away just because they don't like my race. Life is too short and too precious. I put up with a lot of evil mess when you and Janet were growing up. All because I was colored and looked white. That mess came from both colored and white people. No more Cathy! No more!"

Caleb still has his arms around Josette trying to calm her down. "Easy Sweetheart. We haven't left town yet and already you're ready to fight. Don't worry Cathy, nothin' is gonna happen to your mother. We're goin' on a honeymoon not into battle. I agree with her though no one is gonna interfere with our plans. I'll see to that! Now, I have to do somethin' else very important. I asked Josette to marry me but I didn't have a ring. Well, I have it now. Josette honey, will you marry me and wear this ring?" Caleb opens the ring box and everyone gasps at a two carat diamond engagement ring with a gold and diamond wedding band to match. He puts the ring on her finger and they kiss while everyone cheers; everyone except Cathy and Janet. They are still worried about their mother's safety.

Stevie and Timmy are just as surprised as everyone else. They can't believe it either. Timmy pulls Stevie's arm and whispers, "Stevie come outside. I need to ask you something."

"Ok I'm coming." Stevie follows his brother out to the front porch. "What's the matter with you? Why are you dragging me out here?"

"Stevie, If Mr. Carter marries Grandma will that make him our grandpa?"

"I don't know Timmy. Maybe it will or he might be our step grandpa. Something like a step father, maybe it's the same thing."

Timmy is quiet for a few seconds thinking. Then he blurts out, "Then what does that make us? Mr. Carter is white and Grandma looks white. Do we have to change color? I don't want to change color Stevie! I like my color." Timmy is nervous, close to tears and talking fast. If we have to change color, will it hurt? If they use bleach will it hurt?"

Stevie looks at his brother with his mouth wide open. "Where did you get that crazy idea? We're not gonna change color ever. We're gonna stay the same as long as we live. Grandma wouldn't do nothing like that to us and neither would Mr. Carter. I thought you liked Mr. Carter."

"I do Stevie but some of the kids at school said white people don't like us because our skin is black. I'm not black. Look at my arms. I'm brown and so are you. The paper I use at school is white and I don't see nobody that color. I got scared because I don't want to be bleached." Timmy starts to cry.

"Calm down Timmy, don't cry. Nothing like that is gonna happen. Your friends at school are just little kids like you. They don't know what they're talking about when they say stupid things like that. Come on let's ask Mommy or Grandma. Then you'll know the truth."

The front door opens and Janet calls to them. Timmy wipes his eyes fast so his Aunt won't see his tears.

"What are you two whispering about? I saw you with your heads together. Are you plotting something?"

Stevie thinks Janet has overheard them and gets upset. "Oh no Aunt Janet, we were just playing honest!"

"Calm down Stevie. I was just kidding. I didn't mean to scare you. Is something bothering you?"

"No Aunt Janet, we're fine."

"Ok Stevie, you and your brother go play."

The boys run off leaving Janet standing there wondering what's bothering them.

"Maybe it's just kid stuff and I'm uneasy for nothing."

She goes back in the house and joins the party.

Chapter 39

The party is over. Every one has gone home. Caleb and Josette have finished cleaning up and are sitting on the glider on the front porch. It's a moonlit night and they're content and happy with they're surroundings.

Caleb is the first to speak, "Sweetheart, let's spend the night here. We've never done that before and the house is completely furnished. We have everythin' we need to stay. I don't have to go home. Do you?"

"No Caleb, I don't. That's a good idea. I would love to stay. The only thing we don't have is a change of clothing but who cares. Let's say good night to these bugs and go in."

They go in and Caleb locks the front door. When he comes in the bedroom, Josette is standing at the door leading to the flagstone patio. "Come here Caleb look at this. We should have been sitting here. Look at the moon shining on the lake. Isn't it beautiful? The water seems to shimmer and sparkle like a fine diamonds."

"Wow Josette, you're right that's a pretty sight. The people who built this house knew what they were doin'. A lot of plannin' went into where everythin' would be placed." He hugs Josette and says, "We're gonna have many happy years here Sweetheart."

"I believe we will Caleb."

They stand there with Caleb holding Josette in his arms listening to the night sounds of the creatures that live in and around the lake. "Listen Caleb, listen to nature's sounds. They sound like they're enjoying the lake as much as we are. They say if a cricket comes in your house it brings good luck. Do you think one will visit us when it sees someone has moved in?"

Caleb laughs, "I don't know. I never heard that before. You may have told me just in time. I'll be very careful not to step on one if I see it."

It's a long time before they sleep. After making love, they lay in each other's arms planning their trip and the rest of their lives. They talk all night and fall asleep just before dawn.

The next morning Caleb is up first making coffee. The aroma wakes Josette but she stays in bed reliving the wonderful day before. Caleb comes in with a tray. "Wake up Sweetheart breakfast is served."

Josette sits up smiling. "Breakfast? I never eat breakfast this early. I only have coffee and that coffee smells heavenly. Thank you Caleb."

"I'm glad that's all you have because that's all I made. Coffee and toast is all I have this early too. You see, we like the same things."

They stay in bed talking and making love until noon. Then, Josette gets up and starts to look in the draws of the dresser.

Caleb watches her wondering what she is doing. "Are you lookin' for somethin' Josette?"

"No, I'm measuring space. I never looked to see how much room was in these draws. This is a big piece of furniture. I was curious to see how much these draws would hold and they will hold a lot. They're deep and heavy. Before I put any clothes in them I want to line them with the perfumed paper I bought. Come here and help me pull them out.

"Ok, I was wonderin' what those rolls of paper were for. I never heard of perfumed paper. I just throw my stuff in the draw and forget it until I need it. I guess that's why my clothes smell like soap."

Josette laughs and says, "I guess that's why you smell clean but not good. From now on Caleb my love, you're going to smell good too."

When Caleb pulls out the first draw something drops on the floor. Josette sees it first and bends to pick it up. "Wait Caleb, something dropped on the floor. It must have been stuck to the back of the draw." She picks up an envelope. Inside are several photographs. "I wonder if they're of the previous owners. Look, see if you know any of them."

"I didn't meet the owners Josette. I bought the house through the broker but let me see."

The photographs were of an elderly couple with a little girl, a very pretty woman holding a baby in her arms, and many other pictures of the same little girl. Some of them were with the pretty woman. All of them were at the house on the lake. The last picture is of a handsome colored man by himself with the inscription *"My love"* written on the back. Caleb recognizes the man immediately and gasps "Oh my God!"

Josette says, "What's wrong? Do you know these people?"

"Yes Sweetheart, I do. This one looks like Ellie May Potter when she was a little girl. The woman holdin' the baby, I think is her mother. I remember her as being very pretty. It was many years ago. There's somethin' written on the back. It says, *"My beautiful baby girl why did she have to marry that ugly, hateful man?"* I wonder if these older people are her parents. I never knew any of Seth's relatives. This one I recognized immediately Josette. Do you know this man?"

Josette looks at the picture for a few minutes before exclaiming, "Oh my Lord! That is my father. What is his picture doing here? Who wrote *'My love'* on the back? What's going on here?" Josette is beginning to get upset. "Caleb, I don't understand this!"

Caleb tries to calm her down. "I don't know either Josette. Don't get upset. I'm sure there's a simple explanation. Maybe he worked for them and lost it here. Maybe your mother wrote that."

"Maybe Caleb but if my mother wrote that why is it here with these other pictures?

"I don't know Josette but I can ask Seth Potter. He may know since these are pictures of his family. I'm sure there's a very simple explanation. Would you like me to ask him?"

"Yes Caleb, please do but let's keep this to ourselves for now, ok? I guess I got upset for nothing. It just such a shock to see my father's picture here. You can tell it was taken when he was very young." She gives the picture back to Caleb and they leave the house on the lake.

Chapter 40

The next morning, Caleb is at Seth's store waiting for him to open up. He hopes Seth will remember the last time they met at this time of the morning and be off guard. He knows Seth hates him. Caleb remembers those long ago years when Seth beat his daughter senseless just because she fell in love with a colored man. When Seth arrives at the store, Caleb is the one who is shocked. Seth looks like he has aged one hundred years. He's slow moving and he looks sick. Caleb greets him in a friendly tone. "Good mornin' Seth."

Seth doesn't try to hide his hatred for Caleb. It can be seen in his face and heard in his voice. "What do you want Caleb? Why are you at my door this time of the mornin'?"

Caleb ignores Seth's bad attitude and tries to sound friendly. "I found somethin' yesterday you may be interested in and maybe you can help me know what I'm lookin' at."

Seth glares at Caleb but says, "Ok come in." They go to his office at the back of the store and sit. "What is it Caleb? Make it quick I've got work to do."

"I found these pictures and I think I know who they are but only you can confirm whether I'm right or not." He gives Seth the pictures but holds back the one of Josette's father.

Seth's eyes pop at what he sees. "Oh God, oh God! Caleb, where did you get these? These are of my wife and Ellie May when she was little. My wife is holding her when she was a baby. The older people are my wife's parents. Ellie May doesn't remember them. After my wife died they broke off all contact with us." This is too much for Seth. He breaks down crying with his head on the desk.

Caleb sits and waits for Seth to get himself together. He is very uncomfortable in the presence of this man's grief. He was all prepared to have a heated argument with Seth. Now he feels guilty.

After a few minutes Seth is able to talk again and asks, "Where did you get these?"

Caleb tries to keep his voice as calm as he can. "I found them in a house at Blue Mountain Lake. Do you know which house I'm talkin' about? I bought it several months ago.

"Yes, I know the house but I've never been there. My wife's parents owned that house. I wasn't welcome. They came every year in the summer. That's how I came to meet my wife. She had two sisters and a brother. They didn't like me much and tried to keep me and her away from each other. It didn't work though. She married me anyway. You bought their house?"

"Yes, I plan on livin' there after I get married. I'm gettin' married next month."

"Thank you Caleb for showin' me these pictures. I can't wait to show them to Ellie May. I never thought you would get married Caleb. Ain't this a bit late in life to get married?"

"Yeah, a lot of people think that but I'm happy. Josette and I love that house. Do you know Josette Fuller, Seth?"

Now it's Seth's turn to be shocked. "You mean you gonna marry that colored gal from Willow Park who looks like she's white?"

"Yeah, I sure am."

Seth stares at Caleb with his mouth wide open. Then, he yells, "You're a crazy bastard Caleb Carter. Get the hell out of my store!"

"Wait Seth, I didn't mean to upset you. I have one more picture to show you. Can you tell me who this man is? Look on the back and read what it says before you turn it over. Do you remember him?"

Seth takes the picture from Caleb and reads the words out loud. *"My love"*. Then he stares at the picture for a few seconds. All of a sudden he jumps up, throws the picture at Caleb and screams, "They shoulda hung him, they shoulda hung him!"

Caleb is surprised by Seth's sudden fury and jumps up too. He didn't know what Seth was about to do. He looks like he may have a stroke or a heart attack. So he tries to calm Seth down. "Calm down Seth, before you make yourself sick. I didn't mean to upset you. What has you so disturbed?"

Seth sits back down completely defeated. After a few seconds he says, "I'll tell you what happened. Does anyone know about this man?

No Seth, only Josette and I have seen this picture. We don't intend to say anythin'."

"I never thought this would come out after all these years. That man is Joe Winters. He got my wife's sister Ada pregnant. Everybody in the family thought he raped her and they wanted to kill him. She told them to leave him alone. She loved him and she was gonna have his baby. She said they were gonna move up north so they could be together. They never got the chance. Ada was sick the whole nine months. Her family did every thing they could to save her but she died in childbirth. The baby lived though and Ada's mother refused to raise a baby who had a colored father. I think the baby was a girl. My wife wanted to take the baby but I said no. Ellie May wasn't born yet. Ada's mother took the baby to that colored man and never mentioned her daughter or that baby again. The whole family acted as if they both never existed; except my wife. She cried a whole lot then. After my wife died, they refused to have anything to do with me or Ellie May. They had two daughters they were ashamed of."

Caleb sits there in shock. This man is so devastated how can he tell him who Josette is? How can he tell Seth, he's related to a colored woman? He has hated colored people all his life. How can he tell Seth the man in the picture is Josette's father and Josette is the baby Ada gave birth to? How will he take the news that he has a colored niece and his daughter has a colored cousin?

Caleb gets up to leave and Seth asks, "What are you gonna do about what I just told you?"

"Nothin' Seth, I'm sorry I upset you."

Seth isn't the only one upset. Caleb doesn't know what to do. Should he tell Josette or not? Is this one of the trials Josette always talks about that he will have to go through loving her? She has asked him many times if he could stand up to the hardships that will come their way. Now he wonders if she will be able to stand up to the news he has. They promised to be honest with each other. Should he tell her Seth's story or not? He doesn't even know how to tell her.

Meanwhile, Josette has returned to the house on the lake. Caleb is to meet her there after he talks to Seth Potter. She's anxious and nervous. Finding her father's picture in this house has kept her awake all night. Why was the words *"My love"* written on the back? Who wrote those words? What is taking Caleb so long? Just as her patience runs out, she hears his car pull up to the front of the house. She hurries out to the porch to meet him. "I've been impatiently waiting for you Caleb. Did you see Seth? What did he say? Do you have something to tell me?"

THE END